Coco's Story
The Don's Star

Printed ISBN: 9781521566787
Printed in United states of America by Createspace
Published by Michael Powell
Illustrator: Booqla

Chapter 1

Henko, Finland. **1999.**

Markku checked the post-box on the ornate white gates and walked back into the house, visually editing the road for anything out of the ordinary. A daily ritual he had maintained, since his last active 'posting' in Spain, almost 4 years ago.

He found Melanie Preston sitting in the kitchen, a mug of coffee cupped between manicured fingers. Melanie had a new Finnish ID of Kirsten Forsström, which she used for travelling purposes, her 17-year-old daughter, Estela, also had a false Finnish passport, in the name of Rebecca Forsström.

Markku threw the envelopes on the kitchen top and opened the monthly issue of "Six Degrees," a local English Language magazine. He flicked to the rear pages and scanned the small ads. He straightened as he saw the two-line copy for 'PC and Laptop' repairs, no phone number was listed and the email he knew was faked. This was his call.

He glanced at Melanie, she had her head buried in the newspaper and did not look up as he left the room. Climbing to the third floor, he unlocked his private office, connected the secure phone and dialled a number in Germany.

"Hello."

"Hi. What do we have?"

"Meet tomorrow, usual place, 3.00pm."

The line went dead.

He walked down the stairs slowly, deep in thought, but committed to the cause. His life had changed with Melanie, and her daughter, over the last idyllic few years, leaving would be wrench, but she would understand. How long he would be away, was another question.

As he entered the kitchen, she looked up. "I have seen it." She smiled weakly and pointed to the magazine, aware of the coded ads meaning. "When?"

"Tonight, not sure how long. Will you be OK here, or would you like to go somewhere else for a while?"

"We will stay here; Star has her friends and is happy, besides she has an audition next week."

"She has?"

"Yeah, told me as she crept in at 8.00am this morning. She was spotted singing in the bar last night and has been invited to Helsinki for an audition with a new band.

They chatted for a while and started to make plans. The footsteps on the stairs disturbed their conversation, they both turned towards the leggy slim girl with a wild mop of hair. She slumped into the kitchen and sucked air as she collapsed into a hard chair.

" Coffee, urgent. Coffee."

She held her head, as if it would fall off if she released her grip.

"Someone been on the Country Wine?"

"Coffee."

Melanie laughed. "No sympathy from me. Was it a good gig?" Trying to sound as though she could keep up with teen speak."

"Yeah, they went mad, loved our set." She boasted.

"Have you told the band?"

"Not yet, trying to find the right time."

The offer to audition was not for the whole group, just her as a solo singer. It was causing both of them anxiety, the fear jealousy could raise its ugly phizog.

"Who is this impresario who is trying to steal my lovely Star?" Markku joining the conversation, and trying to pave the way for his little bit of news.

"Some old git." She bantered.

Melanie frowned, "You never mentioned he was old. How old, is old these days?"

"Dunno, but he is seriously old, but so famous, he has managed loads of bands, his new band is The Kuntz, from Amsterdam, they are so cool. Funny, but even though he is old, he is kinda sexy."

"Does the sexy old git have a name?"

"Bjorn Free."

Melanie coughed orange juice onto the table. "Oh fuck."

Chapter 2

Paris, France.

The Head Office building for The Sapo Verde Corporation had relocated to Paris, shortly after Coco took full control in late 1995. The business now had 2450 employee's world wide and 5 Managing Directors reported into CEO Michel Palatt, and Group Finance Director, Suresh Patel.

As well as the Coffee Houses, trading under the Bomy brand, they had expanded the "6iX" chain across Europe with a café/bar/restaurant theme. In London they were currently building a replica, of the highly successful New York establishment, in a converted 4 story car dealership. It was set near the Tower of London, midway between the old City of London, and the wealthy new Financial Centre in Canary Wharf.

The clothing tie up with Bjorn Free, which began with a joint venture producing ShitBand apparel, and Bomy jackets, had taken France by storm and their expansion into the rest of Europe and USA was running at phenomenal growth. The young French designer, Dina, had closed her small boutique and concentrated on designing for Sapo Verde under her own label, 'Tomorrow.' Coco enjoyed her youthful vision and appointed Caroline as General Manager for the fashion arm. The new ideas were piloted in Bomy outlets on "fashion evenings," which soon became legendary, with regular magazine and press cover.

The evenings were always arranged at the same time as the monthly Board meeting in Paris, which Bjorn Free attended. His popularity with the trendy young crowd, and the fact he always made sure one of his successful bands attended, always guaranteed a full house. Dina had the controlling vote on all new design and had never failed with her unique blends of racy, but elegant clothes. Production was limited to retain the appeal but often copied by large chain stores.

A daily T-shirt was produced, with a limited run of just 10 per day, each one in high quality material and finished in the colours of the French flag with 'Tomorrow' scripted on the front and rear. Every shirt carried the date of issue and the limited edition number on the sleeve. The first 2 weeks the T-shirts were sent free in Limited Edition glass boxes, to celebrities, mostly good-looking models, or rock stars. The awareness created a waiting list with people able to select their Birthdays or special date, up to one year in advance. It was only just over 3000 shirt sales a year, but the high price and PR value provided a healthy income. Key dates such as Christmas Day, Valentines and key International days were priced from $1000.

Coco's 6th floor office overlooked the famous River Seine. The main building was already overcrowded; a decision to move some departments to a new block had caused a flurry of visitors to her 'always open' door. Most begged her to try and keep the Paris office under one roof and she wrestled with the problem every night. As with any negative for a free mind, there is a positive and she came up with a solution at 3.00am one morning, surprising a sleeping Michel with her shriek of joy.

"We are starting a new division, Hotels!" She bounded from the bed and ran semi naked to her small office on the third floor.

"Good idea, I could be the first customer." A shattered Michel rolled over taking the luxury of the whole duvet as a bonus.

She outlined her plans at breakfast, already 6 pages of hurriedly written notes and drawings. "These will be special hotels, cool, sophisticated almost like apartments but with discreet attention and service. That massive apartment on 59th floors at the 'Top Hat Building,' Coco had renamed it after the take-over; we can make that into the flagship Hotel. Ultra secure, ultra-private and fucking expensive. What other Hotel has a glass walkway 59 floors up which guests brave enough can step onto? A private elevator to the Club on the 9th floor, a gym and a crèche? It will be amazing and gets rid of the stigma of bloody Melanie Preston.

Michel brushed unkempt hair from his forehead. "Is that why we never use it when we are in New York?"

"Not only her, Simon's Cadillac sitting in the middle of the lounge also makes it hard, but yes, the main reason I can't stay there is the reminder of her." Her eyes glassed over for a second but she bounced back into energetic mode. "We can call them 'Top Hat' Hotels." She thrust a rough sketch of the new logo at him.

"Fuck me. From idea, to full blown presentation in 4 hours." He laughed knowing she had already made all the decisions. Decisions they would pointlessly debate with the staff.

"I don't have time at the moment."

He looked blank, "Time for what?"

"Sex."

"Hey that's not fair, I was trying to absorb your news of this wild venture, not seduce you at the breakfast table."

"Bloody men, always about you. I am talking about me; I was thinking out loud. I always feel like this when I have a great idea, but I have n't got the time."

"I could be quick." He smiled, enjoying the upbeat banter.

"I know that!" She skipped past him. "Later handsome, later."

Chapter 3

Helsinki, Finland

Melanie sat in the lounge waiting for her daughter. She was nervous about meeting Bjorn Free, who like the rest of the World, assumed she died in the USS Eisenhower tragedy off Cannes beach, along with her daughter and Jojo Carglinas.

She had always made Estela aware of the reasons for the identity switches and the indigence for security, the only small white lie being her description of Markku's '*career.*'

Estela, or Star, as she preferred, entered the lounge. Melanie gasped at her appearance; she looked every inch the parody of her name, a Star. Skin tight jeans, worn inside out with zips neatly sewn into the pocket design. A brilliant white T-shirt with vivid red lips brushed across her breasts, a small cut pink jean jacket creating a smouldering lascivious look. Oversized Teddy boy creepers, in bright pink suede, added inches to her height, and took inches off her slender waist.

"Wow." Melanie looked at her daughter with pride. "You look fabulous."

"I know." Youthful confidence exaggerated with a model type pose.

"Ready?"

"Ready Kirsten" she joked. "I like the new image Mummy. Not." She teased her again.

Melanie had morphed into Mrs Kirsten Forsström, dyed hair, shaped tightly back and huge 1950's sunglasses gave her a crisp Scandanvian look. She would not watch the audition for fear of meeting Bjorn, or causing another viIconlic arguement with her daughters embarrassment of having her 'Mum' attend a rock audition.

The drive to Helsinki took nearly 2 hours in their new Mercedes G-Wagon. Star connected to music via large expensive headphones, Melanie content to let her mind wander on the empty roads, frequently checking the vista, as taught by Markku.

They found the studio on a street called Aleksan-terinkatu. Melanie parked outside and dropped Star, telling her she would go a nearby multi-story car park and wait for her call. Star bounced her way into the studio, full of confidence, and showing no outward signs of the nerves twisting her stomach into knots. Her Mother's huge 1950's Lulu Guinness sunglasses now perched on her forehead, a trendy signature.

The chic young girl on reception pointed to the stair-way. "Room 4 second floor, just knock and walk in, they are expecting you." She crossed two fingers on top of each other, the traditional sign of good luck.

"Thanks Babe." Acknowledged Star, already using adopted rock verbal.

She galloped the stairway and found the double door marked with a large neatly painted number 4, a red plastic sign read 'Studio only.'

Her knock was strong and she entered the large room. It was empty.

She waited looking around the room for any clue as to what she should be doing. At the far end of the room in front of the huge window was a small two step stage with a microphone set up, a couple of small speakers, 3 guitars and two drums

A side door suddenly opened and three people walked in, she immediately recognized Bjorn Free and half jogged towards him, his face lit up as he threw open his arms in the traditional Bjorn 'welcome.' Elderly hands roamed her figure as he introduced his producer, Sian Methi, an attractive blonde woman. His PA, Anita, had already spoken by phone with Star when they booked the audition, stepped forward offering kisses. "If you can sing as good as you look, you're in girl."

Bjorn joined the praise for her clothing style," Inside-out jeans babe, did you make those, or buy them like that?"

"I just turned a pair inside out one day and made a small adjustment to the pockets." She ran her young fingers across the zips. "It's gonna be my signature." She bragged, confidence high.

"Wow. Cool babe." Anita offered a clench fist and they touched in a friendship gesture.

"Anita, take a photo of the jeans and email it to Caroline and copy Coco."

"Will do."

"OK, you wanna do a routine for us?" Bjorn walking her towards the small stage, as he spoke. "Sian, call the boys in."

Sian walked to the side door and disappeared, returning as few seconds later with 4 young Japanese men.

"Guys, this is Star," Bjorn waved an arm towards her. She turned as he said "Star this is..."

"Fuck me, you're the ShitBand!"

They all laughed, but her composure was fast evaporating.

Bjorn smiled at the embarrassment as she tried to calm herself, "I am going to sing with them?"

"Yeah, they are fairly good." He laughed.

The drummer, Spam, walked over and kissed her gently on the cheek,

"You'll be fine with us." he politely nodded and tapped his drumsticks.

"What we going to do? Do you know our stuff?"

"Of course, I am always singing along with you guys at home." They looked like rock stars, but acted differently to their image, Bjorn's creative imagery their statute book.

"OK, let's run, Made it in the Heart, Carbon Gates and finish with; The Keys are in the Mustard.

"Cool."

Bjorn clapped for silence and lifted a handset attached to the wall.

"You ready up there guys?"

A positive male voice confirmation brought a change of lighting to the room. A small laser of light, beamed through an open window hatch, picking up Star as she stood in front of the famous Band.

"Star we will playback the tapes and video afterwards so as you, or we, need to discuss any changes."

Star felt a shiver of nerves and wished she had not

been so harsh on her Mother attending. She was unaware that Melanie had managed to convince the set manager to allow her into the control unit.

Melanie strained to get a view of Bjorn, but the lighting was subdued and focused on the stage.

Spam walked her in with his intro; words of encouragement from the other band members heightened her adrenalin.

"Two, three!" Spam opened and the familiar thick guitar pulse of, 'Made it in the Heart' thundered around the room. Her first vocal was a little weak but she quickly picked up and roared into the aggressive vocals, bouncing across the floor, full of confidence. The guitarists nodded at her, throwing their instruments high in reinforcement. She was in full swing and Bjorn had already made his mind up before they ended with the moody slang song, "The Keys are in the Mustard."

She stood calmly on the stage, there was a moment of stillness before Bjorn's critical assessment was announced. "Fucking brilliant babe!"

The band circled her clapping arms around her in warmth she had not expected. Spam, the apparent leader, smiled towards Bjorn." She's perfect Bjorn, when can she start?"

Star looked across the room at Bjorn. "Start? I thought this was a new band?"

"Yeah, not quite, we can't go making announcements that The ShitBand are taking on a new member, takes the edge off the promo value."

"You mean I have auditioned for the ShitBand?" She

screamed the words.

"No. Your audition is over. You are in the ShitBand. We will need your parents' consent of course, fucking paperwork drives me mad."

Anita nodded; knowing Bjorn actually meant, "It drives Anita mad."

In the control unit, Melanie made her exit, thanking the crew before rushing back to the car, head spinning with the statement she had just witnessed. She reached the Mercedes as Stars name flashed onto her Blackberry. "Hi darling."

"Mum, I will be outside in 5."

"OK, be waiting." She prayed Bjorn would not escort her to the door.

Melanie eased the Mercedes against the kerb, she knew her acting ability was about to be tested.

Star climbed in, introducing Anita to Melanie through the open passenger window.

"Your daughter has an amazing talent Mrs Forsström."

"Thank you."

I will be in touch in the next day or so." Anita waved her goodbyes and offered a high five to Star. "See ya soon babe. Be inspired."

Melanie turned into the traffic and glanced at Star. Her flushed face not indicating any emotion. "So, come on. How did it go?"

"It was so cool Mum, so cool. Guess who I met?"

"The Pope?"

"Mum, be serious."

"I have no idea, tell me."

"Only the most famous Band in the World, The Shit-Band."

"The ShitBand. Don't I recall they were '*so yesterday*,' as long back as 1995 or '96?"

"I never said that!"

Melanie chuckled, "Let's find somewhere along the coast for lunch, you can tell me all about it."

Star was already connected to her giant headphones and Melanie had no doubt, which band was damaging young, vulnerable ears.

Chapter 4

Copenhagen, Denmark

Markku, now travelling as Paul Hush, an English football agent, scouring Europe for new talent. He was dressed in a Red Adidas rain jacket with a First Chance Academy logo. Dark blue track suit bottoms and white trainers, both with the 3 bar Adidas logo completed the odd look. He carried a sports holdall with a large Nike tick on the side, full of everyday clothes, should they be needed.

The Finnair flight arrived on time at the large hub airport in Copenhagen. He had only his hand luggage and escaped the crowds with ease. His wait for a taxi just a few minutes, he stepped back, allowing 2 cabs to collect people waiting behind him in the line. Once in the taxi he asked the driver to take him to Christiania, the sprawling hippy area of the City.

He offered little conversation to the man, not wishing to get into boring discussions about football, of which he knew very little.

The driver dropped him close to the entrance and was pleased to see a few American tourists waving their arms for a cab back to the night life area. He tipped the man $250; they exchanged eye contact, but no words of thanks, or friendly gestures.

Paul Hush slowly walked past the Kook Café; he turned the corner and repeated the surveillance technique. Waited a few minutes and then entered the café through the rear. He paused, knelt out of sight, pulling the concealed handgun he had collected from the taxi driver; he checked weight and tautened the silencer. He was ready.

The rear door was easily unlocked and he stepped into the scruffy kitchen area. There was no sound of anyone working and the decayed look gave the impression this was either a loss making entity, or a front for criminal activity. The closed sign on the glass door, at the front of the café may well be permanent he decided. Still no sounds, no visible sign of his meet. The gun held loosely in his right hand, no squatting with stiff arms at his end of the fear business.

The Nike bag, left by the back door, in case he needed to exit quickly. He pulled a small funnel shaped tube from his tracksuit pocket, it looked like an inhaler. He flipped the lid, in the same manner as one familiar with the hourly routine of the need for support air. The coating was made of rubber and he skimmed it silently across the floor into the centre of the dull room. There was a small ignition and the room was instantly bathed in bright pearlescent white. In the middle of the room, also holding a gun stood Aaron Milan.

"Now that's what I call professional."

The two 'Brothers in War' slapped hands as darkness returned to the room. Three more men and one woman emerged from the shapes in the wall. Paul Hush was impressed and only recognised Pieter Muller, or whoever he really was.

They were introduced to each other by the name they had chosen, the policy of Gadosh Mitsvah was no one's true identity was ever known by comrades, only to the 4 people at the executive head of the organization. Their only other strict rule was their actions were never related to Political, or Religious groups. Lastly the need to kill during the process was accepted for the betterment of the remaining World. He knew the others were hand-picked, usually wealthy, in order to deter any personal risk surrounding the financial opportunities they may face.

Aaron ushered them all into the cramped kitchen area.

"Ladies and Gentlemen, we have a new agenda. The wealthy Middle Eastern Playboy, Taqi Al-Wahid, and the Middle East stability, over the next ten to fifteen years." He read the wording like it was a Government directive.

Pieter Muller, now using the ID, Tomas Gantlet raised an arm. "What is the latest with the Playboy, he seems to have gone to ground?"

Aaron motioned towards Paul, inviting him to answer.

"I met him 3 years ago in Basra, Iraq. He is a strange man, extremely intelligent but a dangerous individual. He told me at the time he was working on a spectacular event, which would shake the World and bring Islam and wider spectrum of Muslims together as a power group. We," he nodded at Aaron, "decided it would be better to see where this leads. That time has now come; he has invited me to meet tomorrow at 3.00pm here in Copenhagen. Hence the need for Aaron's phone messages calling you all here at short notice."

The room was silent for a few seconds, "What is our strategy with this mad man?" It was the girl, Karin, who spoke. Paul picked up a trace of an Australian accent. She was smartly dressed in what appeared to be an Airline cabin crew uniform.

"Until tomorrow I have no idea." Aaron refusing to divulge the plan, already prepared in advance of the countdown to the attack, or whatever it would be.

"This will be a difficult decision for all of us, the consequences are not palatable to the developed World, and we may well have to accept the sacrifice of some hundreds, maybe thousands, of innocent people, somewhere in the World. Let alone the 2 women we placed within his circle, over 2 years ago."

He paused looking at the faces for hint of distaste; he saw no flicker of doubt, from the group of focused men and women.

He continued, "We feel the attack will be either, Great Britain, Germany, Israel, or the most likely, The United States. Whatever it is, and whatever we decide, we will be aligned to the atrocity, because he needs our help, and we need to appear to be on his payroll. To make sure the future is safe for everyone. That is the dilemma, because we could stem this at source, but it is not our mantra to chop off the head. We need to look at the wider implications around the Middle East, and all of the crazy ones raping these Countries, by persecuting their own people, suppressing women and free speech. They are living the high life in the Middle East, whilst their population are living in the squalor of the Middle Ages."

The room fell silent again. They all knew for Aaron Milan to be so vigorous, this was a serious threat to the World, and the very continuation of Gadosh Mitsvah.

"We meet tomorrow. Taqi Al-Wahid is meeting Paul at the Nimb Hotel. We need full secure cover, just in case, but the main role for you all tomorrow is to make sure he is not followed. They will be amateur in this area so it should be 'a walk,' plus, Paul has the Playboy's trust." He rose and walked towards the rear door; he checked the back alley and invited the group to leave.

As Paul passed him he said, "Just wait a few minutes, we need to chat about something."

Paul hung around as the group dispersed individually at intervals, other than the girl who left with a male member, looking every part the couple, for any interested onlookers.

Aaron sat on a small stool in the Kitchen. "I met with Rani in Japan last week."

"How is he?"

"Business is booming, that Coco woman and him seem to be declaring war on the World with their visions. However, it appears we have a small hitch with ELG-9."

Paul leaned forward, one of only a handful of people in the World to have handled the liquid, and used it in action.

He was interested. "Go on."

"Tests have not been too successful. Remember the big one that caused the massive Tsunami? We were led to believe that the 'bomb' was twice as big as it actually was.

It appears the magnification is far greater than the forecasts they obtained under lab conditions. The reason they reduced the quantity was it becomes highly unstable at a critical volume. The bomb they used was in transport and self-ignited 150 miles from their intended test area. We lost 5 of the team and we only had 12 as the full group. Rani has got a new team together but it has taken time with the security checks and so on. He started again, back to basics you could say. They have been testing minuscule drops on animals. Rats, mice, monkey, cats and dogs. Of course, Taqi Al-Wahid would disappear if he thought this was a dead project, so the need tomorrow is to continue the dialog of trials. If he needs to see an explosion we can arrange a phial test for him, somewhere quiet."

Paul nodded. "Thanks for the cover tomorrow, I don't trust this fucker!"

"I know what you mean. How is the delightful Miss Preston by the way?"

Paul understood the critique behind the question. He had begged Aaron to spare her and her daughter. Because of his love for the girl he, risked everything he had worked towards with Gadosh Mitsvah. Aaron was generous in his response having cleared the situation with the Executive Head.

"Thanks to you, still alive. She's good, the daughter, not too sure, keeps me young I guess. Wants to be a rock star. Barely 16 and wants to be a rock star. What happened to education Aaron?"

"Fucked if I know, I left school at 14, joined the fighting on the borders. Best we leave separately see you tomorrow."

He held out a strong hand and the two men parted.

Chapter 5

Paris, France.

Coco bounced into the morning briefing with Caroline and few young heads of departments.

"My, my, someone's in a good mood." Caroline's suggestive wit towards her boss.

"Sit." She barked. Smile of someone high on adrenalin. "I have the greatest idea."

Everyone held their head in their hands, a comical gesture of another 'off the wall' idea, about to demand hours of extra work for each of them.

"Ha," she enjoyed the sparkling meetings they held every morning, no real grit to the agenda, more a way of boosting morale, and keeping tabs on the current events. "The New York double storey apartment, any of you seen it?"

No hands other than Caroline, who had spent a week at the Sapo Verde headquarters in 1996.

"OK, then we need to rectify that. We are all going to New York for the weekend, unless you are busy, or have something planned?" She knew that would be a 100% take up. We fly First Class, of course and we can bed down at the Waldorf."

Hush descended like mist.

"Wow. OMG and OFO" flooded the boardroom walls.

"Why are we going to see the little flat you may ask? The plan I have developed over the last" she looked at her watch. "5 hours, is for Sapo Verde to open a chain of high end Hotels, starting with the conversion of the 59th and 60th Floors of the Top Hat building. It will be one booking, all-inclusive and horrendously expensive."

No one moved or spoke.

"Now the good news."

The room erupted in laughter.

"This building," she drew circles in the air encompassing the structure." Is too small for us, and our planned expansion."

Eyes brightened and people exchanged looks.

"We are moving to a new larger building, as yet unknown, but hey, I have only had 5 hours on the job. The financial side will stack up because this building will be converted to copy the Top Hat Hotel in New York, other than each of the 10 floors will be bookable in full, sumptuous huge apartment type hotels, the finest luxury, all inclusive, the only Hotel like it in Europe. For now. We plan similar hotels in London, Milan, Berlin, Sweden and Marbella, our spiritual homeland. When people talk luxury hotels, it will be our Top Hat Boutique Hotels, which set the bar."

Mandy, often called by a similar name, for her out of work activities jumped up. "My God, we get to go to New York," she pronounced the 'r' as an 'i' and we get a new office and we all stay together. I'm going out, out, tonight!"

The room laughed as one understanding the female code.

"Right, get the news circulated. And someone get me a fucking coffee!"

She spent the morning chasing every little thought she had. She invited Suresh down after the 'flower arrangers' meeting, as Michel called it, but he knew already, courtesy of her breakfast rant. He was enthusiastic. "My cousin has 6 Motels in California and he makes millions. Sounds a sensible venture to me Coco. I will start preparing some balance sheet info."

After an in-house salad, she sat back in her chair, exhausted from the high of the morning. The Airline tickets had been booked and the excited group spent most of the day boasting to their friends working in 'ordinary places' as they called them.

Her new PA, Delina buzzed. Mrs Boaden on the line for you Miss Cicorre."

It was her first week and the relaxed atmosphere had yet to penetrate the girl's professional etiquette.

"Coco, please. You make me sound so old!" She pressed the connection.

"Ingrid." She yelled her name down the phone. "How are you?"

"Great, just checking in."

"Brilliant timing girl, what are you doing this weekend?"

"Well I have a date with this charming man actually."

"Cancel that girl; we are off to New York"

Ingrid's protest was stamped on by Coco "Look you can fuck the old geezer next weekend, I am taking the girls, and I mean girls, to New York. I can't go alone and Michel would have kittens if I suggested he accompany a bunch of 20 something, over excited French girls to New

York."

Ingrid laughed at the exuberance coming down the phone line. "Look he is not that old, but I guess I could cancel. Hope he has n't wasted too much money on Viagra already."

"Ho. That's the spirit."

"Coco, talking of spirit. You have n't just left Madam Lille's have you?"

"No, no, no. I am flying on tuna salad and Perrier. Come over Thursday night? I will add you to the group. It will be so great to see you."

"OK. Done. I will call with the arrival time. Pick me up in something stylish please. Ha."

"Of course. A Trabant?"

"I have no idea what a Trabant is but sounds good." She hung up laughing.

"Coco buzzed Delina. "I need you to hire a Trabant for Thursday."

"OK."

Five minutes passed and Delina called back. "Er, Miss Cicorre, what is a Trabant?"

"It's a small ant, which comes from the River Trab, filters inland, off the coast of Chile. That's why they call it Trabant."

She smothered her laughter as Delina said "Oh, right" in a somewhat confused manner.

She was still grinning when Caroline walked into her office. "What's up with Delina? Said she's trying to find an ant colony."

Coco could not contain herself and burst into a girlish giggle. "Oh, I had better let her in on my little joke." She buzzed her PA.

"Try 'Googling' Trabant, if you are stuck."

Minutes later the forlorn figure of Delina stood in the frame of Coco's office door, hands on hips and mock facial expression of hurt.

"I suppose you find that funny?" Her 2-person audience belly laughed together.

Calm restored Caroline handed Coco an emailed photo, just received from Bjorn's PA, Anita. "Look at this sexy thing."

"Oh God he's at it again" Coco studied the attractive girl. "Why has he sent this to us, for approval to screw?"

Caroline enjoyed her 'bosses' humour. "Looking at her sex appeal, he probably already has."

Coco suddenly went into parental mode, "I trust you haven't!"

Caroline blushed a little, giving her a reasonable clue. "Might have." She rolled her head at the fond memory of their drunken sex, in the back of his Rolls Royce, following the ShitBand 'After Show' party, 3 years ago.

Coco sighed, "Oh to be young and free."

"Anita said to check out the jeans."

They both leaned towards the grainy photo. "Are they inside out?"

"I think so." Caroline was holding the photo towards the overhead lighting.

"Wow. Neat idea." Coco blinked from looking directly at the light.

"The jeans were the girl's idea, apparently, shall I talk

to Dina and see what she thinks. I like it a lot."

"Yeah, maybe we ride into New York City all wearing our friggin jeans inside out. I had better call Ingrid. Ha, she'll love it. Who is the girl, looks hot and very sexy?"

"No idea, but I have more news you may find welcoming."

"Stop teasing and get on with it girl"

"I replied to Anita and told her we are off to New York this weekend, you know, bit of one upmanship. Guess what, ShitBand is doing a secret one nighter at a small venue off Time Square, and we are all invited."

"Sounds like Mr Free whipping up the marketing again. Is he going to be there?"

Caroline giggled again. "Hope so."

"Pack plenty of condoms then."

"Already packed. Ha. Do you know, the health services have announced a new incentive? Apparently they are offering free condoms for old people."

Coco frowned.

"Yeah, apparently you gather a few old people together, hand them in at the Chemists shop, and they give you 2 boxes of condoms in exchange."

"Piss off you cheeky young tart." Coco pointing towards the door, laughing at the cruel humour of the young. Caroline ran out laughing.

"I just need two or three more of your age and I qualify for 2 boxes!"

Delina looked up with a worried face. "Is it always like this here?"

Coco stood up and danced around the room. What a

day. Junkie high on feelings, she giggled to herself. "Tonight Michel, wait until tonight...."

Chapter 6

Henko, Finland.

Star had been waiting for the call from Anita for 2 days. Sitting by the phone willing it to ring, pacing the floors of every room in the house. Asking her Mother to check the phone was working from her mobile, at least once an hour. All incoming calls were terminated instantly with pleas of "I am waiting for a really important call." Usually followed with a grovelling apology "I don't mean yours is not important."

It was over a late lunch when the phone finally burbled. Star pounced like a cat chasing a loose strand from a wool ball. "Hello."

"Star?"

"Anita!"

"Hi Babe, listen, we want you to come to New York with the band this Friday, we have a secret gig Saturday night and Bjorn wants to use you as a special guest. If the gig goes well, we can build you into the US tour starting next month."

"OFO."

"You better put your Mother on and I will explain the detail and make sure she is OK for you to travel. And," she lowered her voice a little, "We don't allow parents on these trips babe."

Anita spoke with 'Kirsten' for 20 minutes, assuring her she would personally take Star under her wings, for the one nighter in New York.

"By the way, the fee for the gig is $15,000."

"And what would Star's share be." She tried to sound the caring parent.

"No. I mean that is her fee."

Melanie was shocked. "Thank you."

"Remember, Limo will pick her up at 6.00am, Friday."

"OK. Anita, she is young, please watch over her."

"Of course, Mrs Forsström." Anita smiled, thinking to herself, "Like she looks as if she needs any advice in that area."

Melanie sat with her excited teenager and delivered a few 'rules.' Star was elsewhere in her mind and already nervous at the thought of appearing with the band live. Live in her home town, to be more exact. "Far out" she yelled as her Mother's life sketch ended with "You will earn 15 grand from this one gig."

"Cool. Mum. She made no comment on the money. "I have to rehearse the words, to a song by someone called Janis Joplin."

"Is that the *Mercedes* song?"

"Yeah. Who is he?"

"Her actually, the song was iconic, not sure how it fits with the ShitBand sound? Let's jump on the Internet, we can find the words somewhere."

Two days later Melanie Preston resigned herself to walking around the house with headphones on, to avoid listening to Star reciting "Oh Lord won't you buy me a Mercedes-Benz, my..." line time, after time, after time.

Anita had updated her on the format expected of her debut. She would be introduced midway in the performance. She would sing the song solo, unaccompanied by any musical backing, other than Spam intermittently beating his drumsticks above his head. After the second verse the ShitBand would then erupt with her, in a loud high tempo rock version extending the songs length to 9 minutes.

They would have 30 minutes to practise at the hotel. None at the secret venue.

Early Friday morning, a stretched white American Limo pulled up outside their house. Star had been ready for over an hour, and could hardly contain her excitement. Melanie walked her to the car to be met by a burly looking driver in a dark blue suit and matching chauffeurs cap.

"Good morning madam." He directed the words to the teenager rather than Melanie. She was dressed in her signature jeans and had three cases of clothing for a 2-day trip.

She slid into the rear of the car and pressed open the window to say goodbye to her anxious mother. "See you Sunday night. Love you." The smoke black window sealed her young daughter from the World. As the long vehicle quietly pulled away, a tear followed the silhouette of Melanie's nose, trickling onto her top lip.

She slowly walked into the empty house.

Chapter 7

Copenhagen, Denmark.

Trond, now using the name familiar to Taqi Al-Wahid, walked into the Nimb Hotel and asked reception to inform 'Mr Mohammed' he was here, the name Al-Wahid used to travel the World.

The smartly dressed young lady dialled the Suite, booked by Taqi Al-Wahid and his party.

"Of course Sir."

"Go up, 12th Floor, Suite 3. Use the private lift marked 3." She indicated the lift to the right of the reception desk.

Trond walked to the lift and pressed the call button. A video screen opened and a man, unknown to Trond, asked him to step closer to the monitor.

"Please state your name."

Trond talked to the screen and the lift doors opened.

The lift had just 2 motion buttons, up or down. He pressed the up button and the lift rose quickly in complete silence. The doors automatically opened when the lift reached the 12th floor. He walked into Suite 3 to be greeted with a Security check. Two inexperienced minders frisked him roughly.

The older of the 2 nodded, inviting him into the main lounge area.

Sitting beside 3 women was Taqi Al-Wahid; he was wearing white robes and looked very stately. The 3 women, 2 dark skinned and one European departed immediately.

"Welcome." He invited Trond to sit on the sofa opposite his.

"I apologise for the security." He smiled without humour.

"It was no problem, but you need better trained people. He pulled a gun from the rear of his tracksuit. They missed this little gem." He handed the gun towards the shocked Saudi.

"Is this why they call you the Magician?" This time the smile was genuine. "I will thrash them a thousand times and take away their Arsenal season tickets, not that we get to go anymore. Bit unreasonable, when I have promised to finance their new Stadium." His take on English humour amused Trond.

"It's a cruel word, Taqi."

"Indeed it is, living in this squalor is tough." He roared his laugh.

"We have many Brothers within our cause, not just from the Middle East, but as far as Australia, Korea and some of the more forward thinking African Countries. There is concern you appear to have a Jewish name. We need to talk about my plans and what your organization has to offer. Is the new bomb perfected yet?"

"We did not create the name, however, it is convenient for us to use a Jewish label, Israel will get the blame, which suits everyone." It was a gamble of a lie. "As for EL-G-9, it has been successfully tested; I personally took part in one small test."

"Ah, that was you Mr Trond. The McBomb at

Gatwick."

Trond was impressed he knew, slightly concerned how he surmised the make-up of the bomb was ELG-9. He would talk to Aaron later.

"Yes, a small test." He reached in his zipped pocket and removed a lipstick. He sat it upright on the small table. "This was the size we used; it destroyed the whole façade of the building."

"This tiny amount did that much damage?"

"Yes."

Taqi Al-Wahid smiled. "And what size volumes would it take to bring down a building, say, the size of this hotel?"

Trond looked around the room, fearing he would not grasp the size analogy of a Marmite jar. He pointed to a Rubik cube on the floor.

"About that size."

Taqi Al-Wahid picked up the cube and studied it for a few seconds.

"Amazing." He repeated the word as he continued to turn the colours from habit. He discarded it on the sofa in frustration.

"I assume you are in this for the money, like all Westerners."

The hint of arrogance annoyed Trond, but he countered with a little humour. "If you have n't got that oily stuff in your back garden, you have to find other ways of making a living."

Taqi Al-Wahid looked him in the eye and smiled. "Indeed, indeed. So what does a bomb this size?" He pointed at the abandoned cube. "Cost me."

The Bomb itself has no real cost, the costs are the technology to make it work, when, and how you want. Usually remotely, unless you have people wishing to give their lives for the cause."

"We maybe an old fashioned race my friend, we may live in tents and caves, but we are not mad. We leave the suicide pilots to the Japanese Air Force. His laughter was childlike, but then he hesitated, just for a second, like he was thinking of the answer in a written school exam. Eyes scanned the ceiling and he blinked, he scrawled a note on his small pad.

The irony of the coincidence was not lost on Trond. He quoted the cost with a confident voice.

"For the sake of argument, what volume would it take to flatten Buckingham Palace in London?" He clasped his hands together as if in prayer.

Trond felt a sweat trickle of fear, unusual for him, unprepared at the mention of Buckingham Palace, which had come as an unpleasant, possible target. He recovered, hoping the dangerous man opposite, had not noticed his anxiety.

"A half-litre size bottle."

"So the nuclear threat is negated. Downgraded by a small phial of some anonymous liquid."

"Yes."

He fell silent for a few minutes. "Would you like a coffee, or tea?"

"Coffee. With milk." he added, as an afterthought, for his tooth enamel.

Taqi Al-Wahid called an aide into the room. He spoke in Arabic. Trond remained silent, despite understanding every word, including the slang dialect, injected into the conversation.

One of the 3 girls, the European, placed their drinks on the table. She spoke to Taqi Al-Wahid in Arabic and to Trond in English. For the second time in 2 days, he detected an Australian accent, deep in her Oxford English. He buried the fact for later.

The aide departed after the coffee break. "We will be prepared to meet your costs for this item, but we want a sample test ourselves."

"That is fair, we could meet somewhere and I will show you the power."

"No, Mr Trond, we mean a real test. We are going to destroy the American Embassy in Kenya, next week, Monday is ideal."

"Right. That maybe too short notice Taqi, I don't store ELG-9 in my kitchen."

He picked up the Rubik cube. "I am sure you can find this amount by Monday Mr Trond. What technology do we need?"

"We retain the control of the technology; it is so complex it would take 6 months to train even the most competent IT student."

"So we have collusion and trust my friend? Interesting."

"We do."

The discussion carried on and they agreed to meet in Nairobi on Tuesday, giving Trond more time to travel to collect the small phial of ELG-9. He did not divulge the location of Japan.

Taqi Al-Wahid handed back the gun with a smile. They shook hands and the 2 minders retuned to escort him to the lift. They eyed him with suspicion, having been reprimanded by the aide following his conversation with Taqi Al-Wahid. That night the two men were replaced as his private security detail. Both were found some months later, washed up on a small beach in Lammo, across the bay in Sweden.

Trond left the meeting with caution. He could not pick out his own security detail, which showed how competent they were. He neither noticed the deflection tactics they adopted, taking both of Taqi Al-Wahid's men from their 'tail,' after less than a block.

When he was informed, Taqi Al-Wahid flew in to a rage. "Is this the man the Americans call "Superman"? No. Is he human? Yes. You plastic thugs cannot follow him for more than 2 fucking minutes!"

He sat on his bed, waited a few minutes and harshly shouted for the same three women. They instantly appeared in the room. They could see schizophrenic anger in his wild eyes, purple veins sliced into his bearded face. They knew it meant they would suffer for others failures. The options were zero.

"Fuck me now. I want it rough. You fucking harlots."

An hour later, he walked from the devastated room. Harsh looking sex aids, lay abandoned on the floor, the 60-inch TV was still running a violent blue movie DVD. Three attractive girls battered, bleeding and bruised. All three, sobbing uncontrollably.

He calmly called for his aide.

"Clean that mess up, and sort those slags out. The English one can stay, make sure she's ready for tonight, and get rid of the two Arabs, they disrespect Islam."

He walked to the sofa and re read his note. A smile crossed his face, he enjoyed ordering executions, but his thoughts were on another idea.

Chapter 8

Paris, France.

Ingrid Boaden waved to Coco from the back of the airport throng. Her radiant smile, and immaculate style, always impressed the French woman.

They hugged and walked towards the exit. "The Trabant is just through here." She joked.

"Ha, I looked it up; it's a funny little car, a bit like the one they use in Only Fools and Horses."

"In what?"

"Oh my. It's a British TV series, you would n't understand any of it, I hardly do. They talk Cockney rhyming slang, not the real one; they make up anything which rhymes."

"Sounds wonderful." She chided her closest friend." Here it is." She pointed at a huge Military style vehicle.

"Hells bells Coco, what on earth is that."

"It's called a H1 Hummer, they American Military use them all over the World, and now, thanks to Arnie Schwarzenegger, you can buy them for road use."

Ingrid had her hand over her mouth. "It's so bloody big. Who is driving?"

"Me!" Her Goldie Hawn face frightened Ingrid.

"Oh well, here goes." She clambered up to the bus as she called it, not as gracefully as she wanted, but the large crowd gathered around the monster vehicle admired her rear view, with appreciative applause.

The engine fired up with a flurry of smoke from the exhaust, and a choking rumble, as the engine searched for fuel.

"Jesus Coco, can you really steer this friggin' thing through Paris?"

"Generally, they all get out of my way. I am going to re paint it in the Bomy style, use it as a PR tool, like we did with the Cadillac."

"It even feels like you have to shout, what with the noise and the fact you are sitting about 4 rows from me! Ha, this is crazy. Are n't we too old for all this fun?"

"I am still a teenager." She added, "Babe." for effect.

"So what is the New York weekend about?"

Coco explained her latest venture with such enthusiasm it impressed Ingrid, enough to remark, "You know who you sound like Coco?"

"Probably Simon."

"Exactly."

"There is one other reason I wanted you to come to New York, well two actually. These hotels will demand a great deal of input to get the style right, someone who is obsessed with detail needs to be appointed, a person who is confident enough to not have to be constantly asking approval. Someone I trust."

She paused, glancing towards Ingrid.

"That person is you."

"Would you like to be my Development Director? It would mean constantly flying around the World, to develop the size of the Hotel group. £100K salary and a bonus structure. First Class flights and a large clothes allowance.

I would want you to build contacts with Premium products, those which dovetail our style.

"Where do I press the stop bell to get off this magic bus? I must be dreaming, you just offered me a job flying around the World, stupid salary and a clothes allowance."

"I know, fantastic is n't it!" She yelled back across the cabin. "So?"

"That's a yes." She screamed back.

Coco mirrored an old-fashioned Pilot's response with a thumbs up. "Roger that."

"I'd roger anything at the moment." she squealed.

Coco looked blank.

The traffic from Charles De Gaulle built up as they neared Paris. The huge car became a frightening place to be a passenger in.

Ingrid swore, cussed and put hands over her face at regular intervals. Motorist's yelled abuse, as the wide car took up more than a lanes width, bullying small Peugeot and Renault urban boxes into submission. Coco kept her window open, in order to counter with suitable crude obscenities. Usually about the size of their penis.

She was loving her life at the moment, loved having Ingrid back in her fold, another bonus in her jigsaw of life. Deep within her soul, she held an overpowering desire to sleep with her, to touch her in a sexual way. The desire had lived in her for over 20 years.

As they approached Coco's house Ingrid asked what the second reason for her invite was.

"Ah, yes, part two. It depended on part one. I am flying to Japan to meet with Rani next Wednesday. I would like you to come; we can discuss the Hotel group with him, and get some feedback."

"Sounds good. I seem to have started already then."

"Yeah, welcome aboard. Word of caution, we are having dinner at Madame Lille's with my best crew of girls, don't get dragged around Paris by them tonight, you will be in bed for a week!"

"Yes Boss."

The two women avoided the pre-dinner drinks in a nearly bar and went straight to Madame Lille's. Their reserved table section was in the middle of the room and they shuffled their way through the noisy, good-natured crowd.

Ten minutes later Ingrid noticed male diners' heads turning towards the entrance. Madame Lille was busy ushering the crew from Bomy towards their table and, arranged as a bit of fun by Caroline, they were all in paper-thin tight fitting Bomy Jackets, all with their jeans on inside out. They looked so modern and fresh, the youthful ability to re-invent fashion, and have the style to carry it off.

Coco was ecstatic at the gesture and bursting with pride.

Ingrid struggled with French, but agreed to refill their wine jugs mid-evening. The offer of help, from a suave looking Frenchman, seated behind them, was "nothing to do with her decision," she claimed.

The young girls noisily fell out of the Restaurant, egging Ingrid to go back and ask the man for a date. They had chatted during the meal and her alcohol-fuelled confidence was high.

Their persistence was rewarded when Ingrid broke.

"Oh bugger it. Anyone gotta a pen?"

"Mandy always has a pen." Someone joked.

"And a spare rubber." Added another crude wit.

Ingrid stomped back into the bustling room, edged through the crowd toward her new friend, who had introduced himself as Jacque. She was a little unstable but Coco was keeping a protective watch from the doorway. "Jacque!" She shouted above the table banter, He looked up and smiled with his eyes. She passed a scrawled note across the diners. "My mobile, call me. I am in New York for 3 days and then back here for a day midweek, before flying to Japan for a few days."

He laughed at her diary confirmation.

She blushed, not knowing why she had made herself sound like a jet set animal, completely out of character. She added "Adios." As she turned to walk away, pouring more embarrassment upon herself.

Coco was happy, seeing Ingrid enjoying herself. She chatted to Madame Lille as Ingrid struggled through the closely packed chairs, men stood to allow her through, and several women offered smiles and handshakes, reward from the scene they had been part of. As she reached the door she turned, eyes met with Jacque and they waved their goodbyes.

In the street, the girls swarmed around her in a mass cuddle.

"Do you know who that is?"

"Jacque," she slurred.

They laughed as a choir. "That's Jacque Martell." Whispered an excited Caroline.

Ingrid's cold response of "Who's he?" Brought another choir chant.

"Martell babe, like in the drink. His family owns Martell Brandy."

"No thanks, I've had far too much to drink already." She swayed a little and Coco could see she needed rescue.

"Come on Ingrid, come clubbing with us." Mandy, high on the girl power of date fixing.

Coco's warning rang in her head, as further pleas to go clubbing were reigned upon her. She refused as politely as she could, and was grateful when Coco grabbed her arm towards the chauffeured Mercedes.

Chapter 9

Helsinki, Finland.

Star stepped from the long Limo, to be greeted by Anita, and Sian.

"Wow, look at you babe." Anita, bear hugging Bjorn's discovery. "Stefan, bring her luggage through."

Star had not met Stefan before and he introduced himself as the "Tour Manager."

"Don't believe that crap." Laughed Anita. "He's the lackey with muscles."

Stefan snarled towards her in a jovial way, suggesting familiarity with Bjorn's key staff. The chauffeur had placed her 3 suitcases beside the rear of the car.

"Hey girl, we ain't on tour yet, this is a one-night stand." Stefan leered a little, as he chuckled his shock at the volumes."

"Pick it up muscles." Anita was already marching Star into the Airport.

"Jesus, where did you find him." Star enjoying the cosseted attention.

"Oh, we picked him up in London at one of 'Niggers' concerts, he was obsessed with them. Bjorn gave him a job to save him going blind."

Star didn't quite understand the lewd connotation. "Poor boy."

Anita laughed. "I'll explain later."

They swept into the First Class Lounge with a pop

band swagger. Men eyeballed Anita and Star, the mature calm of Sian was broken when Bjorn Free barged her aside, threw Star up into the air, planting both hands on her bottom as she dropped in front of the famous Rocker. "This is Star Buck!" he proudly announced to the galleried businessmen, and women, "My newest superstar, pardon the pun, ha."

Sian and Anita looked at each other. Sian mouthed "Star Buck?"

"Er, Bjorn, we need a chat, leave her alone with the boys."

He let Star escape his bear vice and loudly moaned, "Always bleedin' work, work, work, work."

The suits stayed comatose, males and females still eyeballing the two sensational girls.

Spam ran over and kissed Star. "Come on let's properly introduce you to the boys." He was more animated with an audience. The heady influence and demands of Bjorn she guessed. "This is Aki, Shoji and KO."

The other band members swamped her in cuddles and an exaggerated kissing ritual. Sales had started to fall away and they knew this girl could revive interest in the band. Wild appearance, but already millionaire businessmen, albeit slightly off centre, from the others in the expensively kitted Lounge.

Bjorn sat with his two advisors, as he liked to call them.

"What's up chicabees?"

"Bjorn," Sian spoke a little irritation in her voice." You never mentioned we would call her Star Buck. I assume it is Buck and not your favourite word of similar vowels?"

He laughed. He valued the two girls so highly. "Yeah, Buck."

"Don't you think the 'coffee boys' might have a serious objection, probably pin a Writ on us by 9.00am Monday?"

"Yeah, that's the plan."

Sian and Anita spoke in unison. "Plan?"

"It will get right up their noses, provided they have room, after a weekend snorting their profits" he lifted his eyebrows, adding a humorous cough. "I will fight the Writ, to make sure it gets Star's name on every newspaper front page in the World. Of course, at the 11th hour, I back down. Can't put a price on that kinda exposure ladies."

Two stunned females, sat speechless.

"Then." He held up a hand. "Then." He repeated.

"As you know, I have a very close friend who owns Sapo Verde; we have the joint venture with their 'Tomorrow' fashion house. They also own, the Bomy chain of coffee houses, and are challenging Starbucks, all over Europe, and in the USA. I gracefully concede defeat to Starbucks, and withdraw the naming of our new prodigy, on an amicable basis, obviously settling out of Court and making a public apology. Immediately, we announce Bomy has sponsored Star, the newspapers will go crazy for the story, they love a bit of corporate bickering. We put her in Bomy clothing, and I will talk to Coco Cicorre in New York about using her in an ad campaign, for both the 'Tomorrow' and Bomy brands. Da, Dah!" He ended with a musical themed flourish.

"I need a drink." Anita walked towards the complimentary bar...

Chapter 10

Copenhagen, Denmark.

The group met at the same unused café. Paul, as the group knew him, delivered a detailed synopsis of his meeting with Taqi Al-Wahid.

The bombing test, of the US Embassy in Kenya, was accepted as a necessary part of the wider task facing them.

The meeting lasted just 40 minutes and they slipped into the night, heading for various locations and with a variety of individual tasks to accomplish. Each player had a small team he, or she, could call on. All other contact and direction was through Aaron Milan, who had called them all to the first meeting, once alerted by Paul of the coded message, from Taqi Al-Wahid.

Aaron and Paul remained at the café, hidden from view in the dirty kitchen.

"I slipped a 'lipstick' down the side of the sofa. If you feel we need to terminate now we have 40 hours left before the liquid expands to the dry state. Having said that, I would imagine he will move on tomorrow, so in reality we have tonight, if that is the decision."

Aaron was aware what he meant by 'lipstick.' He rubbed the stubble on his chin. "No. let's follow up with the Kenya plan. I will inform the Executive. If he is planning to bomb Buckingham Palace, it does change the rules a little. The Brits would go mad, if they knew we had prior knowledge and didn't pass it on. Could lead to a funding issue."

The inner workings of Gadosh Mitsvah were a mystery to Paul but he now assumed some of the funding came from a benefactor in the UK.

Paul recalled the hint of an Australian accent and asked Aaron a direct question.

"This is not usual protocol for the organization." His curt answer.

"But this is my contract, and my team. It would be unusual for an Aussie to be so closely involved, more so when I detect two, within 24 hours and both female. I think I need to know the background Aaron, we are all in great danger here, not us, but the people around the World."

Aaron pondered for a minute, itched his growing beard again.

"Ok. You have a point." He looked at his watch. "We have been static for too long, we need to change location. I will call you in the morning and tell you as much as I can."

Paul looked for his Nike bag and found it in at the rear of the kitchen. As he bent down to collect the bag he heard a feint sound from outside the café. He motioned to Aaron. The seasoned pair, instantly alert, both drawing arms. Paul waved Aaron to his right, so as they both had clear aim at the door.

The noise grew louder, two males, both speaking Danish.

The door opened and the two men clattered into the unlit kitchen, inches from the hidden danger of Paul and Aaron. They smelt of alcohol and were tugging at each other's clothing. In the darkness they fell onto the serving island in the middle of the room. The taller man was bent forward as his friend frantically unbuckled his belt, releasing his trousers and pants to the floor. The standing man roughly pulled at his preys' trousers, which succumbed to the force, spilling fly buttons everywhere. The sex was aggressive, rough and loud. Paul caught a brief glimpse of Aaron's face, the disgust registering on the unfortunate intrusion. He ran a finger across his neck.

Two whispering bullets ended the night's pleasure for two young men. The bodies, unlikely to be found for months, in the decaying café.

Aaron left first, openly disturbed by the scene. He had not been involved in 'active' work for some years.

For Paul, just another day, and another two dead bodies, unknown to him, unnecessary dead bodies, in the grand scheme of things.

Paul walked to his small hotel and after running a hot bath, fell asleep quickly. It never worried him to kill.

Aaron called just after 8.00am. Meet me in an hour, outside Tivoli Gardens, it's in the centre. I will wait inside the entrance.

Paul knew to be aware of any surveillance, and used his vast repertoire of caution, to make certain he was alone.

He saw Aaron as soon as he entered, and followed him into the café Orangery. They selected a corner booth and Aaron explained the Australian involvement.

"There is a small, but growing terror group making noises in Australia. They are based on the coast in Newcastle, and have a Yugoslavian heritage. They are openly racist and not dissimilar to how Schwarze Zelle was set up, way back in the early seventies."

"And what are the Aussie authorities doing about it?"

"Nothing as usual, you know how the Politicians' work. No gain, no pay!" He laughed at his joke.

"What are these people calling themselves?"

"ANP. Guess who their financial backer is?"

"I imagine it's my friend, the Playboy."

"Yes he is. Part of his wider plan we are unaware of as yet. That's why we have 2 insiders."

"And one's the girl."

"Correct."

"Christ Aaron, do you know what she is working inside as?"

"Yes, but we cannot worry about that, she can take care of herself, like all of you. The girl at yesterday's meet is her liaison, she lost her for a few months but we were lucky to regain contact when they returned to Europe. It appears he has been in Afghanistan, living in a cave for the winter. There has been detailed list of names, which she was able to provide, from her time with the visiting terror chiefs. Some men tell anything during of hot sex with a young woman."

"And the other insider."

"A Lebanese girl, not one of the favoured 'group' at the moment, but making a name for herself with senior officers."

"And these two are within our non-payment criteria?"

"Of course."

Paul shook his head. "We have some really dedicated people within our ranks. Such commitment, I could not begin to imagine the sacrifices they have made. I am not sure I could it."

He stood to leave.

Aaron held out a hand. "I know, we are proud of them, the information we gain is vital for the long term objective. One more thing. The Executive are keen to meet with you. We have a few loose ends to tie up. I will be in contact."

Chapter 11

New York, USA.

The ShitBand's arrival at JFK Airport was meant to be a 'secret.' The PR opportunity was too much and whilst nothing like the mania days of a few years back, the fans turnout was as noisy as ever, the fashion still worn by the faithful.

The Press had begun to ignore the band and this was reflected in no organized Press conference. A caustic comment from a lone freelance hack was dismissed by Bjorn with "this is a private visit."

Star strutted through the walkway side by side with Anita and Bjorn, just ahead of the band members and Muscles with the rest of the crew. Sian remained at the rear of the human train, as if there, to pick up the pieces.

They arrived at the Michelangelo Hotel, a few minutes' drive from the secret venue for tomorrow's performance.

Star walked into her top floor Suite. "Is this all mine." She asked Anita, who had led the way.

"All yours babe. Enjoy. Dinner is booked for 8, meet in the bar. Dress edgy. You are on show."

"I will try." she said with a raunchy giggle.

Anita was waiting for Star with Bjorn and Sian in the hotel bar. Bjorn had been there an hour and was getting louder by the minute. A group of Japanese businessman, sitting on the next table. had recognised him and been plied with drinks by the manager of the top Japanese band.

Bjorn's eye for any new business contacts always alert, his capability to consume alcohol in vast quantities, and at reckless speeds, legendary. The group had matched him drink for drink for over an hour, from their glasses of wine and small beers, they had graduated to 'slammers,' courtesy of the wild Swede. Happy to select each round of drinks by moving along the top shelf, at alarming speed, it was Bjorn's game, a game he called 'Line Drinking.'

They were smiling, alcohol flushed smiles as Bjorn slammed down another purple coloured liquid,

"Whose fucking turn is it?"

Haro stood and bowed, he called the waiter over and slurring a little asked for "the bottle behind the purple one," as selected by Bjorn moments earlier.

The waiter walked back to the bar pointing at the purple bottle.

"No, one behind purple bottle."

The confused waiter removed the purple bottle, indicating the 'one behind the purple bottle' was the reflection on the mirrored wall, which formed the bar design.

Haro could n't quite grasp the man's English and said again, "Yes, one behind the purple."

Bjorn stood and in mocking Japanese accent bellowed, "Hero, hero, hero, we gotta *ploblem* 'ere".

The group burst into laughter, amid much back slapping for the unfortunate Hero.

The tired waiter prepared another round, removing the 9th bottle, the next in line to the purple bottle, which was oddly called Blue Curacao. Bottle 9 was named Green Chartreuse, and looked equally disgusting. By the time they reached the 12th bottle, a fierce white spirit called Arak, Bjorn had the whole group singing, 'If I were a rich man.' The famous song from 'Fiddler on the Roof', originally performed by Topol.

Several guests were complaining about both the singing, and Bjorn's offensive language.

Anita and Sian sat chatting, oblivious of the vocal carnage caused by their boss. A few hardened drinkers had now joined the Japanese choir, although the track remained stuck on 'If I were a Rich Man.' An Irishman with a flowing beard and black pipe had taken the lead role. He energised others, encouraging new 'members' around their corner of the bar, to join in.

Without any notice the singing stopped, as if a conductor had drawn his baton, ending the song.

Anita looked up at the silence, and followed hungry male eyes towards the bar entrance.

Standing alone at the door was Star. She was wearing a fine, see through black mesh dress with one-inch width diagonal stripes running down the length. The dress was skin tight, mini short, and clear to anyone, she had no underwear on.

The diagonal stripes concealed her body sufficiently so as not to expose anything too offensive. Long flowing dark hair and high 6-inch Jimmy Choo heels, completed the look, a fine balance between 'whore' and 'pop star, usually dependant on your gender.

Anita elbowed Sian, "That' what I call edgy."

Bjorn yelled something, a little obscener.

The smiling choir ordered bottle 16 from the top shelf.

Chapter 12

Okinawa, Japan.

Rani Delaware had blossomed in the top seat at Ashtimo. Business had expanded with the many joint ventures with Sapo Verde in Paris. Coco Cicorre, the owner of the French company kept in constant touch and they operated a transparent system between the two huge companies. It included the exchange of staff for 6 month periods to give both groups the unique opportunity to experience other cultures and working methods.

He regularly visited his mentor, Mr Seonitno Toyo at his house and today was not exceptional.

They sat in his wonderful gardens and drank tea in the sunshine. Rani gave him a synopsis of the previous month's accounts, and their new ventures, mostly at the planning stage. This was a voluntary action, but one the young man valued the added input of an experience businessman, a businessman who loved the company, he had stepped down from 3 years ago.

"Coco Cicorre is coming to visit next week; I know she would like to meet with you if you are free."

"Of course, she is a brave and outstanding woman, let's have dinner one evening here in the garden." He smiled and stood indicating he wanted to walk amongst the fragrant gardens.

"What is the latest on ELG-9?"

"We should finish testing in a month or so Sir. The

tiny drop tests on animals were completed over a year ago and are a little inconclusive. It is hard to figure the expansion ratios, as you know, and the new staff has yet to reach the technical levels we attained before the disaster 3 years ago." Rani was uneasy with the progress, and the demands of the project, but was fully committed to the endgame. "I will keep you in the loop Sir."

"Thank you. Everything in the garden is fine. Ha, do you remember that film?" He smiled a weak grimace of past memories. "I have forgotten the name of it."

"Not sure Sir."

"Never mind Rani. I will get you a copy. Would you mind if I visited the lab to talk with the technical boys?"

"Of course not Sir, ELG-9 is your baby; I understand and appreciate any input. They will be delighted to see you."

"Tell them I will drop by at 9.00am tomorrow."

The haste of the visit shocked Rani and he thought he had just been 'played' by the clever old man.

"Will do Sir. They will be up all-night cleaning the place." He nervously laughed.

"Are you OK Rani, you always look a little stressed to me, maybe that's your natural look?"

"I am fine thank you. A little upheaval on the private side of life. Randolph has gone back the USA, he couldn't make his mark in Japan, never mastered the language and I work long hours. It just drove us apart."

"I am sorry; he seemed a nice young man." Toyo nodded to the short man walking behind Rani.

"Hisoka will show you out. Let me know the date for

dinner, I look forward to that."

Rani shook hands and bowed before walking along-side Hisoka. He made a note to train himself in the art of dismissing people, politely, when you had reached the point of no further business.

"You learn something new every day." He told himself.

Chapter 13

New York, USA.

Air France First Class cabin crew struggled to entertaining such a young group of females, attractive good-looking trendy girls, who had partied from lift off, to landing, and seemed impervious to customary alcohol consumption rules. The starchier first class clients seemed to warm to the group and the atmosphere, far from the normal polite reserved behaviour; was loud, people changed seats, and generally joined the party.

Mandy pestered Ingrid on the man from the previous night in Madam Lille's. "He is so rich." But she was more interested in a restful flight, before their night out with Bjorn Free.

Coco introduced herself at every opportunity, passing out business cards saying "They are better than lottery tickets, call me." Champagne has a lot to answer for on flights.

Stretched limo's collected the group and they headed in convoy to the Waldorf Astoria. The banter in both cars was in slang Paris, and the drivers both felt they had travellers from another time zone. They were dressed oddly, hair was weirdly styled, language was odd and so rapid, and they laughed, they laughed all of the time.

The same shock awaited the Reception area of the hotel as the group swarmed around the desk, checking out the young males in an obvious statement of confidence.

Other guests stood in awe studying the dress code and styles of the attractive group.

Coco and Ingrid suddenly felt very old.

She called the crew together. "OK. Time is 10.00am locally. Meet at 12 here and we will go to the Top Hat Building, which is not too far."

The girls all cheered and raced for their rooms, shrieks of laughter disturbing the gentile atmosphere.

12 noon the group assembled in the foyer. Everyone had changed and the effort to look 'hot,' was clearly a joint decision.

Coco turned to Ingrid, "If this is their day wear. God knows what they will wear to the club tonight."

Ingrid looked embarrassed. "Jacque just called."

"Oh my. And?"

"Having dinner on Tuesday, is that OK with you."

"Hell woman, you don't need a 'pass out' when you are at my house. Coco turned to the girls, "Girls, Ingrid is in the lead. 1-0." She had heard the girls had a league table running.

"Coco" Ingrid eyes wide open. "It's dinner, that's all."

Mandy stepped forward," That counts as a goal, he buys you dinner, somewhere really, really expensive, so you are in control. You have an open goal as they say. I mean, don't tell me you won't wear your sexiest under-wear.

"Of course."

"There you are then, why, if it's not for a..."

"Mandy." Coco beamed a 'stop it' face.

They bundled out of the door singing "1-0 to the Innnner-grid, 1-0 to the Innnner-grid."

Outside, two frightened looking doormen, opened the limousine doors and took the banter on the chin, not understanding the crude jibes anyway.

The girls were a little subdued on the short drive. "Everything is so big." said Caroline.

"Yeah, like Delina's arse." yelled someone. Shrieks of laughter filled the car's interior.

"Hey come on girls, she's new, and she is back at the fort, taking all your calls. Be a bit more polite." Coco not wanting the new girl to feel out of sync with the crew in the two limos.

They pulled up outside the sixty floor head office. "Wow." Became the general quote, spoken with a respectful whisper, rather than raucous predictability.

The high-speed lift whisked the party to the 59th floor. The ambience had resided to normal, as the sheer scale of the apartment became apparent.

Coco took centre stage and told them the history of the 21 foot Cadillac, sitting beautifully polished, in the centre of the main room.

We originally used the car as a PR tool to create awareness of the bar, which was the first "6iX" outlet. Later we cut the roof off and used it as a DJ's centre point in "6iX Le Club," the first Sapo Verde venture into nightclubs.

Later the car was shipped back to the US. West Coast Customs stripped it back and restored the car to its original Sedan de Ville status, that of a hard top. The car was fully refurbished and craned onto this floor during construction. It can probably never leave, but has been valued at a quarter of a Million US dollars. It's a fancy sofa really." she joked.

They walked up the sweeping staircase to the second floor, mostly bedrooms but with a glass roofed games area, looking out across New York. A series of expensive telescopes gave the girls the opportunity to gaze at the neighbours. Back on the 59th floor, she slowed the pace, "And now, the one feature which makes this apartment so unique, and, which gave the building a new identity, courtesy of local New Yorkers, who nicknamed it the Top Hat building, from day one."

She walked to the air lock door and opened the heavy metal frame, they stepped into the inner chamber, once closed they were tightly packed in and already showing signs of nerves. The temperature control in the tube could be varied from ice cold to tropical. Coco had asked for ice cold and when she opened the outer door the bite of arctic air assaulted the group.

"Follow me." She stepped onto the glass floor and tried not to look down. The girls followed, several screamed at the view below them and clung back to the safety of the chamber. It took a while for some to move but randy Mandy led the way with a "hey ho, it looks safe to me."

Others followed but most contented themselves with watching from inside as scared friends edged around the tube. At petrified snail's pace it took some of them nearly an hour. Coco touched a panel on the wall and the clear glass tube turned green, another flick and it turned red, white and blue… "We use that on American Holidays," she told the excited audience.

Back in the safety of the apartment Coco asked them to consider what they would add to make their Hotels stand out. She also announced the appointment of Ingrid as Development Director. Ingrid acknowledged their applause.

"This is amazing Coco, did Melanie really live here?"

"Yeah, office downstairs, restaurant and bar-café downstairs, shops, gym, crèche, all downstairs. Not need to go anywhere.

Downstairs the offices were closed for the weekend but they took a quick look inside the Club and wandered the shops, attracting admiring looks from the sales assistants, as they in turn, studied the French girls' clothing.

They followed Coco into "6iX" the massive café–bar on the bottom two floors. Their reserved pod left the dock and swung into the middle of the floor, high above the other guests. The room was packed and a long line snaked the frontal area waiting to enter.

The chatter amongst the girls was about it being, "Like you were on another planet," they loved it.

Ingrid spoke quietly to Coco. "You know Coco, despite her disgusting behaviour; Melanie has managed to take Simon's dream to another level. Shame she got involved with that gangster family, she has a real creative talent."

"I have often wondered, why did she turn so sour, why spend your life as a mistress, OK, he had money, and power, but could you screw someone that ugly?

"I married David."

Her joke fractured the dismal topic; they fell against each other, both crying with laughter.

Coco had the same intense feeling to touch her.

Chapter 14

Henko, Finland.

Melanie sat alone in her house. The wind had gathered pace all day and now remorselessly battered the windows, and tall trees outside.

She was feeling low. She had not heard from Star, and although she knew it was not on the agenda, neither had Markku called.

She poured another glass of Chilean red wine, her fourth in the hour.

The mood changed when the house phone rang.

"Hello."

"Hey, fancy a night in?"

"Markku, where are you?"

"Parked outside, some fucker has double locked the gates!"

She screamed her delight. "That fucker was me, and yes I am a fucker tonight, we are alone for once."

She raced outside, hair flaying in the high winds, she clicked the gate lock, to release the safety system Markku had installed. He drove in and leapt from his perched seat, into her arms.

Reunited lovers walked arm in arm, back towards the house.

They sat in the kitchen talking; she poured him the last glass from the bottle and took another from the rack. "Easy girl" he teased her.

"If you are not up to it mister, then I have a bottle of liquid Viagra upstairs."

"Jesus, is that made in liquid form as well."

"Well they normally call it Gin, but It works for me, makes me as horny as hell."

"Wish you had mentioned that a few years ago."

He grabbed her in his arms and lifted her off the ground, she squawked loudly." Take me sexy man, take me."

The house phone interrupted his return banter. "Oh, that might be Star"

He dropped her and she raced to the phone. "Hello."

"Mum. It's me."

"How's it going?"

"It is unbelievable, I have a stage name, I am going to be called Star Buck"

"Oh nice darling, he's full of ideas that old git isn't he. Hope he has n't flirted with you too much?"

"Well. He doesn't really mean it Mum."

She wished she could explain that, "Yes dear, he bloody well does," but levied her reply as positive as she could. "I know."

"Mum, we have rehearsed, and it went great. I am on in about 3 hours' time, think of me." She started to cry.

"I love you Mum, and Dad."

"Take care, and good luck." Melanie, now fighting tears as well.

She replaced the receiver.

"She just referred to you as Dad, said she loves you. That's the first time she has acknowledged you as Dad."

Her eyes watered and she slowly walked towards the kitchen. She returned clutching the second bottle of red.

"Come and cuddle me." She sank into the huge comfortable sofa.

Markku's body was complaining about the delayed expectancy of sex, but he knew the moment had passed.

"I'll take a shower and be right back." He leaned over and kissed her forehead.

"OK, you hungry."

"No, not really."

Chapter 15

New York, USA.

The small Club was usually the venue for American fringe Comedy. A two-minute stroll from Times Square, it was located in a narrow alley, the type so familiar to TV addicts. Only a scratched white door identified the Club. Its bizarre name tattooed on the top half, 'Closing Soon.'

A famous New York comic had established the Club 47 years ago, when he opened his club, friends would jive with him, "Be closing soon, Errol." The original name of 'The New York Comedy Club' faded away within 2 weeks and the institution, 'Closing Soon,' which still exists today, was born.

When Errol died in 1968 his friends displayed their humour writing, "Errol Peterkin - Opening Soon," on his headstone.

The three Black Chrysler Voyagers turned into the alleyway leading to the Club. They all gasped at the scene as Police tried to control a large crowd, trying to force their way into the free gig.

"Oi, fuck me girls, someone's let the cat out the bag." Bjorn revelled in the way you could drip feed secrets these days, drip fed into a storm of interest.

The Club was already full. 300 lucky ShitBand fans screaming their heads off at the support band's thundering music. They took their final applause as they finished their 4 song set.

They were a new band from Philadelphia, called the Spunk Hermits, another one of Bjorn's growing academy of offensively named bands.

The crowd bade for the ShitBand, the small, hall like venue, exploded as they walked onto the tiny stage. Despite the low number, you could not hear above the screams, and sing along fans.

Their set was limited and after 20 minutes they eased back with a slower melody, to set up a calmer atmosphere for Star's debut entrance.

She was standing in the wings. No ShitBand uniform, her own signature of inside out jeans. Or 'turn outs' as Anita had renamed them. Her top was a tiny soft leather bikini bra; her favourite 50's creepers in vivid pink enhanced the tight jeans. Wild black hair teased out, widening her stance, gave her the full on rock chic look.

Anita smiled "Go shock 'me girl."

On stage, the lighting faded to dim. Spam was highlighted at the rear of the group; a single beam of light chased his raised arms, as he tapped sparkling chrome drumsticks above his head.

Bass guitar, KO, next to be picked out by a single beam.

"Please welcome our special guest tonight. Star Buck!"

The fans paused as one, not recognising the name, or the ShitBand format, they were so familiar with.

Anita gave her a gentle push. Her heart was racing; she was sure she had forgotten the words.

Spam tapped again as KO's beam subsided.

Her time had come.

Star strutted onto the stage; the fans raised the volume, easing her nerves. She reached for the microphone, yanking it aggressively from its stand. Spam hit the third tapping sequence.

It was now.

She opened her voice with the over rehearsed lines, the stunned audience hushed silent. Some lightly joined the words providing a childlike choir drifting across the room. It was a surreal moment.

As Star ended the first verse all 4 members of the ShitBand were picked out by single high intensity light tunnels. The heavy guitars energised the crowd and Star reacted by upping her tempo. The sound was amazing as the whole club came together as one with the band. All 4 on stage were now full force with the words, backing up Star. The fans were yelling now, no low moody hum of words, full on rocking.

Above the bedlam you could still hear her distinctive voice as Star took command of the audience. The extended song ran over the 9 minutes as they lost their way in the crescendo of sound, and excitement. They finished to rapturous applause and unrecognisable screamed pleas.

At the edge of the stage, Bjorn whispered to Sian, who had the running order clip in her hand. She nodded above the volume and moved closer to try and attract Spam's attention. Ever professional, he knew to eye check with her after every track.

Before he could deliver the message from Sian, Star turned to the band and said, "Let's do the keys."

Spam shrugged, looking sideways Sian also shrugged, but added thumbs up. Bjorn and Anita grinned at each other.

The 'Keys are in the Mustard' has just 2 lines, 11 words to be exact. It is believed to be a hidden code, connected with drug use and the origins are spoken of as legend.

An eccentric English Poet, Mickey Woods, part wrote the song sitting on the top of Table Mountain, in Cape Town, South Africa. He was stoned out of his head at the time and missed the last cable car off the mountain. He spent a bitter cold night, huddled against the café walls as the famous 'blanket' enveloped the flat-topped mountain. He refused pleas to finish the song, claiming that night, "I died several times, and these were my final words."

It became known within music circles as, 'Mickey Woods Unfinished Rock Song. 1976.'

Bjorn had secured the rights to the song and The Shit-Band had a Platinum hit with their version in 1995.

Star blew the crowd away as lead on the number, teaming up with KO and Aki in duets, using the words in an outrageous and highly provocative performance.

Bjorn was speechless at the side of the stage, the support crew, and club staff had stopped to watch her sing. It was a moment of group adrenalin as she finished the number. The 4 boys clapped her off stage and the crowd yelled for more.

Bjorn swamped her as she left the small stage. "Come here babe, you were fucking fabulous!"

She accepted his open arms and bedded herself

against him. For a second their eyes met, and she thought she would kiss him, not a touch kiss, or peck, a full on meaningful kiss. She calmed a little, but eyes had spoken to each other. She knew she had to experience his reputation. They touched hands as they parted as she was engulfed by others.

Anita let her fly for the moment, but noticed Bjorn had sat down, a little drained from the evening.

"You need a pick me up?"

"Need fucking Viagra more like it, shit she's hot!"

Anita winked. "Yeah, she's hot alright."

Chapter 16

Newcastle, Australia

Rossco Jedelavic ran the ANP from the rear of a small tavern in the coastal town of Newcastle. Their membership, just 15. A single criteria to join, you had to be descendants of Yugoslavia.

Outside of the 15, the hooligan element now totalled 400. Mostly disillusioned ex pat offspring, who never felt accepted into Australian culture, as much as other Europeans were. It was easy to manipulate young minds towards a useless future. Blame it on their ethnic background, the staple diet of reasoned argument, a powerful tariff used all over the World.

Their activity had been low key and mostly contained to angry talk at heavy beer drinking sessions. Taqi Al-Wahid's network had been known to be searching for a poorly run organization, to front their longer-term activity in Australia. Taqi Al-Wahid saw the Country somewhat independent of Europe and the USA, a perfect breeding ground to develop radical thinking...

It was no surprise to Rossco, when a female aide contacted the ANP and made them promises of wealth beyond their imagination. He received regular drops of small firearms and transport, but was now meeting Taqi Al-Wahid for the first time, at their tatty headquarters in Newcastle.

As the group filed into the room, at the rear of Amy's

Tavern, they showed signs of nerves. They sat in 2 rows with Rossco Jedelavic and Bilac Meliovlic, seated on the hall stage, facing them.

The door at the far end of the hall opened and a tall man in a neat suit entered. His long beard at odds with his immaculate tailoring. Behind him walked two men, also in Western dress, both black suits and muscle.

"Good evening gentlemen. I am Taqi Al-Wahid."

The group applauded and whispered amongst themselves.

He spoke for 20 minutes, telling them he was impressed with their progress, with such limited resources and manpower. He promised more funding and then turned to the payoff, by way of their involvement.

"We have to train your people, we can arrange for a training camp in Pakistan, all expenses paid. We will teach the natural leaders amongst you, to become trainers in their own right. We will give you the expertise to cause real discomfort to the Government, and to make you a powerful lobby for the rights of badly treated immigrants. I will talk in more detail once I have discussed these plans with Mr Rossco and Mr Bilac. Needless to say, this is confidential. My organizations are powerful and you must not betray us. To demonstrate this commitment to you and to convince you to obey our rules we have arranged a small display of our capabilities. Please join me outside."

The room rose as one, low voices beginning to worry, and ask new questions.

The filed out to the small field at the rear of the tavern.

Taqi Al-Wahid raised his arms towards the sky. "Where is George Branson?"

"Here." A slim man stepped into the pale light, flicking shadows from the moons glow.

"And how long have you been a member George?"

"11 years Sir."

"Why do you have a non-Yugoslavian name?"

"I am a carpenter and there is prejudice against foreigners with names the locals find hard to pronounce, my kids suffered with bullying at school so I changed it, almost 5 years ago." George Branson was shivering, not from the cold, but the intensity of the eyes, burning into him 5 feet away.

"Not so patriotic then George?"

"I, er."

"No, is the answer you are fumbling for George!" Taqi Al-Wahid's eyes closed like a laser beam about to cut metal, as he raised his voice.

"Bring the girl!"

In the shadows a muffled scream could be heard, the group turned assuming it was a wild animal, a common sight in the small town.

A torch beam opened and a third man in a black suit manhandled a naked girl towards the centre of the group.

"Terri, oh my God, what have you done to her?" George screamed out as her recognised his 15-year-old daughter. Her eyes were bruised and she was bleeding from her groin area, spider shape red lines of blood ran like veins down her thighs. All 3 black suited men had drawn weapons.

"George, I have to make my point, you see, you are not committed. You joined the opposition to better yourself and I imagine this is a little game to you, just a laugh, and a chance to rap in the old language a couple of times a week. Before we came here I raped your daughter in your matrimonial bed, we made your wife watch. She is an attractive girl; did you know she was a virgin? I like fucking virgins George; it is part of our religious belief."

The girl sobbed, lying in the centre of the circle of frightened men trying to cover herself.

"I want to kill you George, so as the others know I am serious. But I will spare you; I will spare you because I have taken something irreplaceable, your daughter's virginity. Everyone here understands, they will remember her body, every time they see you. Your wife will be waiting for an explanation at home, that maybe painful for you to defend."

His message was clear to the group. Their lives were never going to be the same, or their own, ever again.

"Rossco, Bilac, we need to talk. The others can go. Please do not even consider asking for Police help. If you do this miserable little town will be flattened immediately."

He turned and walked back to the tavern.

The silence palpable.

Chapter 17

Henko, Finland.

Melanie grabbed the phone at the second ring. She could hear a cacophony of background noise.

"Star"

"Mum, mum, it was fantastic, just oh, so cool. Can you hear me?"

"Yes darling it sounds wild."

"Hold on Bjorn wants to speak to you"

"Oh no darling I..."

"Hello, Kirsten is n't it?" she recognised his voice and trembled trying to create an accent.

"Ya, Kirsten."

"Listen, she took the place by storm, even took the script apart to suit herself, fucking amazing girl. She is gonna be huge. We need to meet; I will get Anita to send you tickets to Paris in a couple of weeks if that's OK with you, all expenses paid. Gotta go, the Star wants to party."

Melanie could hear loud screams and people on a high experience in the background, but her daughter did not return to the phone. She hung up.

Markku looked up from the TV.

"Everything hunky-dory?"

"I am old." She sat down and sighed. "She is having a great time."

In New York, Bjorn walked away with a niggle in his mind. "That voice, she reminds me of someone?"

Chapter 18

New York, USA.

Coco and her group found Bjorn and his crew in Barrington's Bar at the Michelangelo Hotel. The venue had been booked for the after show party, although it looked as though Bjorn's penchant for young girls, had stretched the entrance qualifications somewhat.

He saw them coming and rushed towards Coco as always, grappled her sideways telling her "she was the sexiest woman in the room."

"Yeah apart from me and Ingrid, and some of the waitresses, the others are all girls; you are too smooth by far Mr Free.

She knew he found rejection hard to counter and had teased him for many years.

"Where's my wonder girl, Caroline?"

"Here." She tapped him on the shoulder and jumped into his embrace kissing him rather seductively. "Good to see you Bjorn, as always." A hidden message passed.

He had forgotten Coco already and surfed Caroline's body with lustful energy. "You look horny."

"That's because I am." She laughed poking his stomach.

Coco wrestled her away and he moved on to practise more seduction techniques, on others, keen to meet the rock legend.

Mandy was busy claiming an equalizer. "In the toilets

at that grotty club."

"Who with?" Asked Caroline, the official scorecard person.

"Oh blimey I have no idea of his fucking name, just grabbed him from the madness when that girl came on. It was so hot, and so quick, I loved it."

"OK. 1-1. everyone, she waved in the air, Mandy has equalized."

"What a surprise." Bounced back from within the exuberant dancing

French girls, Ingrid was in the middle enjoying herself. She pushed her way back to the bar joining Coco and one of the band members, Spam.

She spoke into Coco's ear. "Jacque had called twice more; I feel like a sixteen-year-old."

"I'll get you one, hang on." Coco joked.

The night was long and boozy, not until 5.00am did the room start to clear.

As Mandy left clutching 'Muscles' and one other member of the crew, she yelled over her shoulder "3-1. 3-1."

Coco gathered the remaining girls, other than Mandy the only other 'missing in action' was Caroline.

Dina interrupted the headcount with a drawled slur, she's not missing in action Miss," She joked. "She's getting some action with the drummer Spam; I saw them slip away just now.

"3-1-1 yelled the team."

Coco shook her head; Ingrid was also missing but she didn't worry about adults. "I'll say goodnight to Bjorn, jump in the cars and I will be out in a minute." She flagged the girls away.

Bjorn was sitting on a sofa with Star." Have you two been introduced?"

"No. I thought you were brilliant tonight Star, absolutely brilliant"

"Thanks babe" she said in cheeky rock language.

Coco agreed to meet for lunch the following day, to discuss a few business matters, Bjorn had raised.

Anita walked over and extended her arm toward Star, "Come on, I promised your Mum you would be in bed by dawn, it's nearly here."

Stars eyes flickered and she hauled herself from the shared sofa. "OK. Babe." Anita wagged a finger at a sullen Bjorn. He growled back.

Coco walked to the front exit, she realized her walking was not too stable; she grinned at the reception staff and tried to appear in control. She opened the door to a chilly blast and looked for the cars.

The heavy coated doorman asked her if she "needed a cab."

"Have they gone without me?"

"The French group?"

"Yes."

"I am afraid so ma'am, sounded like they were off to another club."

"Oh no." She laughed. "Rain check the cab. Thanks."

She turned and walked gingerly back to Barrington's. Bjorn was still on the sofa, now the last one in the room.

"Hey, come back for another drink gorgeous."

"They left without me." She looked at him, so trendy,

so successful but only once married, and then only for a few weeks. She had heard a thousand stories of his prowess in bed. She was tempted, and felt a little lonely.

"What you gonna do."

"How much would you pay to fuck me?"

He shot up in the leather sofa. "What!"

"Don't answer that." She held her hand palm facing him. "I want a bit of discreet fun."

"Am I dead, this must be heaven? Sex with you, after all this time."

"Shut up, and start walking..."

Chapter 19

Sydney, Australia.

The four men sat in the Hotel restaurant, eating a tourist version of Lebanese food.

"Azul, you were brilliant today, even I thought you were that fuck Taqi." The tall elegant man, now devoid of the expensive suit and beard, was casually dressed in Hawaiian Shirt and oversized beige shorts. He laughed.

One of the others chimed in. "I bet she was a good tight shag, eh Azil"

They all laughed.

"No my friends, I said she was a virgin, because I felt sorry for the sad old Yugoslav man. She was really enjoying it you know how horny girls are when they have their period."

"Oh disgusting."

"Well, I say she was enjoying it until brother Zaheed here, wanted to join in."

"Zaheed. Is this true?"

"Not entirely my friends, I didn't want the girl after Azil," He screwed his face adding, "Goodness knows what deceases he has, I wanted the Mother."

"Oh, gross."

"I didn't, the bitch feinted as I took my pants down."

More raucous laughter followed.

"Here boys," the four Moroccan friends leaned toward the centre of the table. "Who paid us to do this little job?"

"Who cares, anyone who wants to pay me 10 grand to impersonate' Mr Al-Wahid' I am up for it, especially when they supply hot young girls as part of the deal. Look fellas we 've all been here 4 years, and so far we have fuck all to show for it. Bigots', some of these Aussies, I even have a bit of sympathy for the ANP guys."

Zaheed disagreed, "Yeah, get real. When do we get paid?"

"Tomorrow, we meet by the harbour, 10.00am. Even the girl who arranged this is super cool. Maybe our luck has finally turned Aussie into wonderland?"

The attractive girl jogged up to the group at the meeting point outside Walt's Bar and Grill, a tired façade, at odds with the picturesque harbour. Beside her, a heavily panting French bulldog eyed the 4 men, his busy nose seeking nerves.

"Sit Cosmo." The muscled dog flattened himself against the pavement.

Her accent deep Australian and loud, "Here yer go mates." She casually handed Azil a plastic supermarket bag.

He looked inside; it was crammed with loose notes. His face beamed.

"Count it if you want, but I can guarantee it's all there. Fancy doubling yer money? I have another small job for you guys."

Her physical attraction, in tight Lycra running gear, was part of the lure, and she knew how to suggestively pose, to keep their brains from thinking properly.

A chorused "Yes!" earned admiration from her spotter, hidden amongst the yachts.

"She's good" Aaron Milan said to himself.

He saw the group exchange pleasantries and moved away.

Karin Moore, unaware she was on 'active test,' from the Executive.

Chapter 20

Okinawa, Japan.

Mr Toyo was greeted at the Research establishment with the respect he had built up over the last years.

He smiled as staff members bowed to him and returned their kind words.

He talked at length with the head of ELG-9 development adding his sadness about the loss of the team members in the tragedy. Igo Namicho was in charge of the overall laboratory, reporting in to Rani Delaware.

"What are the reports on the animal testing showing us Igo?"

"Not a great deal Mr Toyo, the effect of minuscule drops is nil, you have to grow the dose substantially, and then, as it reaches the critical mass it expands but we have found it hard to contain, or calculate the rates by volume. It is unstable at this point."

"Did any of the animals show any side effects whatsoever?"

"None, sir. We increase the dose by just 15% and 4 rats died and 2 dogs, it is beyond this dosage that we are working to find a control mechanism."

"I see. What are the oldest animals to survive, that we have tested"?

"Some are three years old now."

"And looking healthy."

"Yes, Sir, they all look in excellent health."

"Thank you. Igo. The facility looks to be run very efficiently, well done and keep pushing for answers. It is a project very close to my heart."

"Thank you Sir. I will find a way, I promise."

They bowed and shook hands.

Mr Toyo returned to his large house and called Aaron Milan on a secure phone.

Chapter 21

New York, USA.

Coco stirred and blinked at the darkened room, she felt very dry, but the realization she was not in her own hotel suite worsened, as a grunt behind her startled wakening senses.

She looked over her shoulder to see the forlorn figure of Bjorn Free. Wild hair ruffled in every direction, his features tired and old.

"Oh shit." She moaned to herself," What have I done."

She tried hard to piece the end of the long night together, she recalled drinking in the Club, dancing and chatting to God knows who in the Bar, and then snatches of flashbacks, romping madly with the old man of rock. He stirred and opened bleary eyes.

"Oh grief," she thought, this could be the familiar, horny man syndrome, waking up with an erection, wanting to fuck again. Not necessarily me, but anyone, just to alleviate the build-up of testosterone.

He turned to face her and smiled. "Come here sexy lady." He pawed at her naked body and stepped a leg across her, he was strong and she moved her hand to try and stop the mounting action. Her fingers inadvertently touched his erect penis as she did so, and her internal reaction was of shock. She didn't let go but explored the breath of his manhood. He rolled back, flat on the bed and she felt so aroused, she climbed on top of him, pushing her eager body towards him, she cupped her hand under him directing his throbbing ache into her. She screamed out as her entered her. "Oh, God! Bjorn."

He arched his back and thrust forwards in a strong virile manner, old hands, experienced hands, caressed her breasts and she floated into another World as he ejaculated violently inside her, she felt the full motion blow inside her as she collapsed on top of him. She groaned, sucking for air and aching for more of the same.

An hour later, the bedside phone rang. He leaned across and answered. "Thanks Anita, be down in a minute."

"Sorry babe gotta go to some live breakfast Radio Station interview. Listen, sorry about last night, I was too tired and had too much to drink, maybe we can make up some other time?"

She wondered what the hell he meant, but went with the flow. "Just a one nighter Bjorn, I am in a relationship."

"He's a lucky man."

He climbed from the bed naked; she studied him amazed at the size of his penis. "Has that been inside me?" She shuddered at the thought, but swam in the sexual experience.

He left within 10 minutes, remodelled back to Rock Star status, and off with the very sexy Anita. She wondered how big the club she had just joined was, and who did it include?

After he had departed she hurriedly dressed and walked downstairs. Thankfully the doorman's shift had changed and she didn't have to mumble a reason why she stayed overnight. The Yellow Cab drove through quiet streets, she stared out of the window at tall buildings and the mirror effect they produced, her cab a flashing yellow odd shaped tube, passing smoky glass. Her mind wandered to Michel and she felt bad, it soon greedily reverted to Bjorn and the amazing sexual high. It was worth it for the experience, she silently bargained with her own inquisitive ego, good girl brain making the excuse of 20 years confinement.

They pulled up outside the Waldorf Astoria, she glanced at her watch, "Thank goodness it's early, at least none of the girls will spot me creeping in like some tart."

She paid the scruffy looking driver, who grunted at the tip. She was annoyed at his attitude.

"Look I have just had to fuck a miserable old man to get that money, so cheer up, things could be worse."

Her accent, purring French, but in a Hollywood way. He grinned and looked her up and down. "Dream on arsehole." She silently spoke to herself with a lecherous grin. "Hell, when do I grow up?"

Her self-inflicted humour received an equally huge smile from the doorman.

She entered the foyer, screams erupted from the open plan breakfast room, she looked over, and the full complement of team Bomy, cheered their boss. "Come over Coco."

She breathed in heavily." Be cool, find a reason, find a reason. Attack, yeah, attack."

"Hi girls, you're up early."

"We only just got back, this city rocks man." It was Mandy, always life in Mandy she mused.

Caroline stood up. "Updated figures ladies"

Coco blushed; this was going to be difficult.

"We have a new leader. Dina is claiming an unsubstantiated 4. Mandy is on 3. Caroline 2 and Ingrid by default i.e. not in her room, has scored again making her on 2 already. We have 4 others on one including the boss. We also have guest entrant, Star, she's on assumed score of 1.

Coco looked shocked, "But Star went to bed before me, I saw Anita grabbed her and take her upstairs, she's only 17.

"Yeah, but she was all over Bjorn last night, and he had his hands all over her, she was loving it. We realized we had forgotten you and went back, but you had gone. We went up to her suite and no one was there so we checked outside Bjorn's room. The noises coming from there were unbelievable, so we credited her with one point, although the effort sounded worthy of a 2. Ha"

Coco was on the defensive and went for deflection. "How did Dina score 4 when she left the bar 4 hours ago on zero?

Dina stood to conduct a slightly erratic statement about her claim on the scoreboard of love. "We left the bar and decided to go onto a Club. The nice doorman, recommended the Sapo Verde club and so we all ran riot in there. They would n't let us in at first, but Toni Shawe was there, with Ester and Ginny from the New York office and they saved the day. It was full to the rafters and the manager came over and said we could have a free tab as we were

Sapo France. He was so cute I had him in his office, just a quickie, but it counts. He then introduced me to a group of Basketball players, man they were so big, er tall I mean, not that, you know?" The group cheered. "After I went back to their place and the four of us got down, as we say in Paris." She shrieked "They were big there as well" She pointed to her groin and screamed her laughter, holding her hands apart like a boasting fisherman.

The conversation stalled and smirking faces looked towards their glamour boss. No one asked, but she could hear their thoughts.

She bottled it. See you in the foyer tonight. Don't be late. She could hear the cheers as far as level 2 in the elevator. "God what have I done."

She reached her suite, hung a 'Do Not Disturb' on the door and stripped naked. She admired her body in the full length mirror and told herself, "It would be OK."

She soaked in luxury for an hour, mindful of her meeting with Bjorn; she called Ingrid's room to see if she would come with her, for support and, because she was uncertain how she would cope.

Ingrid answered sounding a little groggy. "Yes?"

"It's me."

"Coco."

"You OK, you sound a bit tired."

"Bit? Am I in the middle of some experiment on human behaviour of older women, these last 3 days have tested me, I feel wrecked, these girls can party."

"I know I have just seen them downstairs, they have only just got back."

"Me too."

"What!"

"I went to a club with one of the sound engineers. I can't tell you the rest over the phone."

"I think I know, the scorecard has you down as 2 points."

"Huh, is that all, it feels like more. I ache in the love passage."

Coco laughed. Meet me at the roof terrace for coffee in half an hour, I have to tell you something. Have to."

" Oh, make it 15 minutes then, it sounds exciting. I have some other news as well."

Chapter 22

Nairobi, Kenya.

Markku had enjoyed just one night at home before flying to Japan to collect a Marmite size bottle of ELG-9. He had also picked up a new supply of mobile phone bombs. Boarding the onward flight to Kenya he was stopped and searched, the cleverly disguised gun, hidden in a box marked Alfa high intensity Internet aerial, and the 6 different designed phones back up his credentials as Development Director for Sony Ericsson, all passed inspection, as he knew they would.

He checked into the Panari Hotel close to the Airport terminal.

Two hours later his mobile rang. "Welcome to shitsville." The unmistakeable voice of, the Playboy. "What hotel are you in?"

Markku lied. "The Sarova Stanley."

"Fine, we will pick you up around 7."

He checked his watch, 4 hours. He reassembled his gun and added the bulbous silencer. At the same time, he activated 2 mobile phone bombs and set his laptop to link with the ELG-9. The 'spare' AC Adapter disguising the deadly liquid content.

At 5.30pm he called reception and asked for a taxi to go to the Sarova Stanley Hotel. He changed into lighter clothing; the heat outside the air conditioned hotel was intense and draining.

The taxi ride was stifling, the battered Peugeot's air condition had failed many years previously, but the unattractive driver lied for the 10th time that day, banging the cars instruments, "Bloody AC unit had packed up, sorry Sir." Markku read the lie and cranked the door winders as far as they would go. The heat intensified as they approached the City centre.

"I should leave this lazy bastard one of my free mobiles phones." He joked to himself, as sweat stains appeared on his crisp blue shirt.

He entered the hotel and found a cool area in the bar, ordering an ice cold beer, with a "Hurry the fuck up," desperate eye message to the smiling barman. He still insisted on the training formalities; wiping the bar surface, carefully placing the neat little mat and flipping the top from the beer with a flourish. He was about to dispense the entire bottle, into the frost chilled glass, Markku had a near obsession with topping his beer glass himself, preferring to add more froth as he drank. The anticipation boiled over and a firm hand reached across the bar top, he grabbed the barman's arm and coldly said.

"I'll do it myself, thanks."

The barman looked into steely eyes and dropped the charade.

Markku gulped the first mouthful, always so rewarding when you are thirsty.

"Hello Trond."

He turned to see Taqi Al-Wahid behind him, a huge smile across his face. He resembled a modern day Jesus in his flowing robes.

"You look a little hot."

"Little is an understatement." He returned, shaking hands with the tall thin man. "Drink?" He pointed to the bar.

"Gin and Tonic, lots of ice, please."

Markku raised an eyebrow at the alcohol request, which the Middle Eastern man picked up.

He laughed, "We are all human Trond."

"Double standards." More like it, he thought.

They finished two more drinks and Taqi Al-Wahid suggested they leave to tour the City.

"I trust your vehicle has air conditioning working Taqi."

"Of course."

The Mercedes was brand new and surprisingly Taqi Al-Wahid jumped into the driver's seat. No other visible back up was noticeable, which Markku took as a compliment.

He drove the Mercedes around a few tourist hot spots before he indicated the US Embassy. As usual, the security was vivid and blatant, armed soldiers stood by the gates, they all looked menacingly at the Mercedes.

"Usual bollocks." said Markku. "Pull over."

"What here?" A concerned tone in his voice, almost a frightened edge to his words.

"Yeah, right by the gates."

As the expensive car slowed the attention went up a few notches and hands waved them on. Markku ignored their instructions and stepped from the car. In a formal Swedish accented voice, he asked, "Can I take a picture of the building it is really beautiful."

Two soldiers, in crisp uniforms, looked at each other for an answer to the tourist's request.

"OK buddy, but make it quick."

"I will get my camera, thank you so much."

He had left the car door open and a nervous Taqi Al-Wahid was trying

hard to be invisible. Markku fumbled in his small brief case, producing a camera and a rectangular shaped black coated accessory. He turned toward the building holding the box to the light, convincing the guards he was a photography geek and needed a light meter reading before his "quick" shot.

They exchanged bored looks.

He took 4 quick snapshots and then turned to the first soldier, again

emphasising his accented Scandinavian vocals.

"Where is the Swedish Embassy?"

The frustrated solder replied, "Sir, I have no idea, you really gotta move that automobile. Have a nice day."

"Ah, sorry, thank you for your time."

Markku walked towards the open Mercedes door asking in a loud slow voice, "Driver do you know where the Swedish Embassy is."

Taqi Al-Wahid was close to panic. He breathed his words quietly, "Get in." The Mercedes pulled away, a little faster than Markku would have preferred.

"What the hell were you thinking of, that was madness."

"I was n't *thinking* anything I was planting a bomb."

The car swerved slightly.

"Steady Taqi. It's game on. We're active."

Unseen by the two bored Soldiers; he carefully wedged the 'light meter' on a small ledge, at the side of the reinforced concrete barriers.

"I will never play cards with you Trond."

He smiled, two compliments in one day from the Playboy, was a bonus.

"What time tomorrow do you want to set the bomb?"

"Let's say, just after prayers, seems acceptable under the circumstances."

"OK. Call me when you are ready, I will meet you somewhere for a million-dollar IT training session.

"Ha. I like you Mr Magician."

"Are you sure you are not confusing me with Paul Daniels?"

"Who?"

Markku was beginning to like the man.

Chapter 23

New York, USA

The roof garden bar was empty; Coco found a table overlooking Central Park and ordered coffee for two, from the efficient waitress. She always enjoyed the Americana language of 'politeness' for the first three or four days of a visit, beyond that it began to irritate her.

Ingrid breezed into the calmness of the bar and walked towards Coco, a broad smile on her face.

"My word, you look pleased with yourself."

Ingrid smiled, "I am bursting to tell you about the last 24 hours in my life."

"And I am anxious to hear, go on."

"He's coming tonight."

Coco removed her sunglasses. "Who is?"

"Jacque. He is flying here, arriving tonight and, if OK with you I will stay here until Tuesday, and fly back on his Company jet, in time for our Japanese trip."

"There you go again, asking my permission to run your own life."

"It's so exciting; do you think I am crazy?"

"No, but you must have sold him a benefits package of 'all night kinky sex' to get him flying here, after a mere 20-minute chat up session."

They laughed together, enjoying banal conversation.

"And your news?"

"God, listen this is awful. I drank too much last night and suddenly found myself alone with Bjorn."

"Oh no, you didn't!"

"I did!" she squealed loudly like a 15-year-old telling tales of her first sexual adventure.

"And. Are the stories true?"

"No, it's bigger."

Ingrid covered her mouth. "Did anybody see you?"

"Not sure if even Bjorn remembers anything, I don't."

"So, maybe you didn't then." Ingrid trying to alleviate the worry it would cause Coco.

"No, but I could n't stop myself this morning, it was just an amazing experience, no love, or anything, but one hell of an erotic experience."

Ingrid waved to Benise, the waitress. "Two glass of chilled champagne please."

"How do you feel about it; Michel I mean?"

"Have n't come to terms with it yet, trouble is I have this meeting with Bjorn and I feel a little awkward, to say the least."

"Come on, it's not like you do it every day"

"No but I bloody well would n't mind!" Coco's worry expunged with a friend's support, and a joke "What was this with the engineer?"

"The good looking tall guy, it was a crazy moment and I just thought, what have I got to lose?"

"At least you made the scorecard."

The wine arrived and thcy toasted the 'Naughty Girls US tour'.

"Hey, I have an idea, this Jacque man thinks you are some International jet setter, why don't you stay at the apartment, that should impress him somewhat? She picked up her Blackberry and dialled Toni Shawe to give her instructions.

"Yes it would impress him, impress him into thinking I will be an easy lay."

"This of course, is exactly what you want." Her laughter drowned with Ingrid's high pitched "Coco!"

They left the Hotel and met Bjorn at Michelangelo's Barrington bar. He looked up and Ingrid noticed his eyes sparkled toward Coco, she also noticed Coco had the same eye virus. She was a little shocked.

The meeting passed quickly and they discussed many of his fashion ideas. Coco asked Bjorn to look at the apartment and outlined her plans for the new Hotel group, together with Ingrid they jumped in a taxi, for the short journey to the Sapo Verde building.

Bjorn was ecstatic about the apartment and eulogised over the style and views. "Fuck me; this walk around tube is like having a funfair in your home!" He managed three steps before he said, "maybe another time."

She made a playful ageist comment, which he found amusing.

"How much is gonna cost?"

"$100K per week."

"When do you launch?"

"4 weeks, not a lot to change here, but this will be a blueprint."

"OK, I'll book it for 6 months, enough bedrooms for a

couple of bands; I am here so often, it may even work out cheaper. You should have a massive launch party here, my PR mob can get busy on the details and if you can weigh in with your input, it will give your venture terrific exposure. "Tell you what; I will have Star as the guest entertainment for the party."

"Deal" said an energetic Ingrid.

Coco smiled "What happened to seeking my approval?

They agreed to meet in Paris as soon as Ingrid and Coco returned from Japan.

Coco wanted to touch him so badly.

Chapter 24

Nairobi, Kenya.

Markku arrived at the narrow street, half a mile from the American Embassy. He found the gaudy looking Jambo Terrace Bar easily. He took a seat with his back to the wall.

He checked the time 3.00pm. He was booked on a flight to London at 7.00pm, his holdall of clothes by his side. He was keen to leave the capital before the panic evolved.

Taqi Al-Wahid had still not arrived at 3.30pm. His mobile chimed.

"Hi."

"Sorry, I am delayed, be with you soon." In the background Markku heard an echo, it sounded like an airport tannoy announcement.

He shifted on his chair, immediately folding his laptop, leaving enough cash on the table to cover the two beers. Instinct, told him he was in danger. Walking slowly, he hailed a passing cab. 200 yards on he told the driver to stop, shortly after crossing a set of lights. He gave him $10, apologising for the short journey. He waited until the car had disappeared and walked up a dirt side road.

He found a small unloved Isuzu van, carefully checking for any onlookers, he smashed the driver's window, climbed in and had the engine running in under 8 seconds.

He drove back towards the Jambo Bar. Outside were 4 Police vehicles and a heated discussion was taking place with the waiter, who was pinned against the wall, hostile policemen were slapping his face, demanding answers. The other clientele carried on drinking, as if it were daily routine.

Markku was angry. "So Taqi, you try to set me up." He said the words out loud; angry he had not been more careful. He parked the scruffy van and climbed in the rear amongst pipes, and what appeared to be plumber's paraphernalia.

He opened the laptop and connected his high resolution mobile. He tapped in the sequence and cursed as his fingers shook, the anger was affecting him. He climbed back into the driver's seat and started the engine.

Jambo's bar had been chosen because Taqi Al-Wahid wanted to be close enough to witness the force of the explosion. A few seconds passed and his van violently rocked as he heard the signature 'boom' in the distance.

He smiled to himself. 2 hours ago he had telephoned The Daily

Nation newspaper from a pay phone and in perfect Arabic had told them there would be an attack on Kenyan soil, by Insha'Allah, within 4 hours. He repeated the message in accented English to 2 Radio Stations.

He had exposed the blame.

Markku drove the van to the airport and parked in a multi- story car park, leaving a small mobile under the passenger seat.

He entered the airport and noticed the Police and security had already upped the threat level. A glance at the flight information pointed him to an attractive girl at Gate 12. She smiled but looked concerned. A Police officer looked over her shoulder, carefully checking the well--worn, red British passport, and his return BA ticket.

He remained calm and offered no more than a weak smile, as if just another bored English businessman, heading back home.

He was handed his boarding pass and 70 minutes later, boarded his British Airways flight to London.

The smiling cabin crew girl handed him a beer and a small packet of peanuts. The 'bite' of the first beer tasted even better than usual.

He was pleased to be meeting Aaron in England; the Taqi Al-Wahid development had changed things...

Chapter 25

Paris, France.

Coco arrived before 7.00am to find her new PA, Delina already busy in her office.

A neat pile of post lay in the middle of Coco's desk with a typed list of people to call back, and a guide to the reasons. She was impressed.

"How was the weekend?"

"Great thanks," her guilt still churning emotions within her. Michel had been very attentive when she got home late Sunday evening, but she faked tiredness, for the first time since meeting him.

The girls had all arrived on time for their usual weekly meeting, which turned out to be verbal replay banter of the weekend fun.

Coco was a little quiet and Caroline picked up her mood. When the others left, she stayed behind.

"Are you Ok?"

"Exhausted." Was her softly spoken response. "How do those girls do it?" She shook her head. "Do they behave like that in Paris?"

"Like what?"

"You know, all these boys, threesomes, casual sex and so on."

Caroline burst out laughing. "OMG, that's not true, the league is a bit of fun. Believe it or not, Dina is still a resolute virgin, her having a threesome lives in her fantasy brain. We talk about it loudly so as to shock anyone listening, it's so funny. Hey, we even scored you a point, and none of us think you are going around shagging someone on a one-night stand. That would be ridiculous."

Coco focused on her eyes, not sure if she should be offended by her remark, but desperately searching for the truth.

The brief stand-off of silence was broken by Caroline.

"That's how *we* deal with it." Caroline shrugged, holding open palms toward Coco. "Playing away has different rules. *It never happened.*"

Coco smiled, relief pungent. The colour returned to her cheeks.

"That said, can we talk about my pay increase?" A huge grin adding to her model looks.

"Out!"

Caroline raced from her office laughing.

Chapter 26

London, England.

Markku stood in line at the Black cab rank, patiently waiting his turn in the most strictly controlled taxi environment in the World.

A constant stream of clean taxi's filtered through the cab lane, scooping up passengers in an orderly and well organized fashion.

He jumped in, asking through the small divider window, for The Lanesborough Hotel on Hyde Park.

The chatty driver made good time and he arrived just after midnight, UK time. Apparently 'Spurs' had lost again, and the cabbie wanted the manager fired.

In the morning his bedside phone rang with his pre-selected wake up call. He had been up 2 hours already.

He walked downstairs, crossed the busy intersection of Hyde Park corner and on towards Piccadilly. At Half Moon Street he turned left and knocked on a non-descript door marked, The Fox and Ruby Club. An additional typed message, held in place by three drawing pins, on curly and torn A4 paper, added, 'Members Only'.

The door opened and a woman in her early fifties invited him in. "Mr Hush."

"Yes."

"Mr Milan is in the breakfast room; he is expecting you.

The interior smelt of stale food and was not attractively appointed. He assumed it was for this very reason they were meeting here.

He saw Aaron Milan sitting facing him, the other man had his back to Markku.

As he approached Aaron stood up and pulled another chair to make a three seat table. The other tables were all empty. The second man turned and introduced himself with a firm handshake, but no name offered. In Markku's World, names meant very little.

The unnamed man was part of the 5-person Executive and Aaron's direct link.

They discussed the action in Kenya but were unaware of the Taqi Al-Wahid situation. Markku was praised for his actions and for completing the task so efficiently.

"The Press are already convinced that it was Insha'Allah, your calling cards were very effective and we got what we desired, but why has he jumped ship?" Aaron was anxious for the full detail and they spoke for nearly 2 hours.

The Executive remained very quiet through the discussions, but introduced a note of interest to Markku.

Aaron had been short listed for the Executive as a member was due to retire due to illness; they in turn unanimously wanted to appoint Markku to their liaison team, reporting directly to the Executive. This was 12 months away, the end of 2001, but he readily accepted the challenge.

Aaron added a sour note that the 'English' girl, working inside Taqi Al-Wahid's group had failed to make contact after Copenhagen, not unusual but worrying, given the bail out in Kenya.

He asked Markku to meet her liaison girl, the one at the recent meeting, to see what trace they could effect." She's been in Australia, tidying up a couple of loose ends; if you can meet her there she has small amount of ELG-9 and a target, similar OM to the operation in Kenya. I will give you full details within the next 2 days.

Aaron indicated the meeting was over. Markku left by the rear exit, which led through an untidy narrow alley, onto Piccadilly.

Aaron and the Executive member sat chatting for a while, mostly about general matters, before the Executive asked about Melanie Preston.

"Does he know?"

"Not yet."

He nodded, "OK, I will leave it to you."

"Thanks, it will work out in time."

"Just remember, *you can't buy time.*"

Chapter 27

Paris, France.

Ingrid stepped from the big Audi at the entrance to Coco's large house. She was hidden in her bedroom on the second floor, but watching intently as the couple said a polite goodbye.

She also noticed Jacque Martell glanced back as the chauffeur pulled away. Ingrid did not return the compliment.

Coco rushed downstairs, opening the door as Ingrid fumbled in her bag for the key.

"Well?"

"Wait, let me through the door first, goddam it!"

Coco grabbed her bags and rushed her through to the kitchen. She held up a single finger to her mouth and whispered, "Michel is home."

The friends shared a bottle of chilled Chablis and Ingrid recounted her few days with Mr Brandy.

"Oh, is that a slip of the tongue?" she asked, smiles all round in the girl's chat.

"Nothing happened, he was the perfect gentleman." Ingrid looked serious.

"Oh yeah, you sound like Caroline." She told her closest confidant of the '*It never happened*' conversation, adding things with her, and Michel, were not so good.

"And Mr Free?"

"Sent me 3 dozen red roses to the office!"

"Oh hell." Ingrid smothered her hands across her face." That has to stop."

"I know, my new PA, Delina, was a brick, she told everyone they were for her, some ex-boyfriend trying to win back her favours."

Ingrid pointed upstairs meaning "How is Michel." without speaking.

Coco waved her hand in a gesture of "offish." They had no made love since her 'tired' rejection on the Sunday.

"You had better turn him on tonight."

"Not sure I want to."

Ingrid looked at her face. "Coco, it was a one off, don't waste this wonderful man for Bjorn, he has probably slept with 3 others since then."

"I know but there is a deeper connection with the past and I am unsettled. I'll get over it." They touched glasses as Michel walked into the kitchen.

"Fancy a meal out ladies."

They both answered "Yes," but meaning "No".

Chapter 28

Sydney, Australia.

Markku had spent just one night at home with Melanie and his newly focused daughter, before boarding a flight to Sydney, Australia.

He arrived reasonably fresh from his long First Class flight, casually dressed as the Football Academy manager, Paul Hush.

He was met by a Qantas Airline's complimentary chauffeur service, which whisked their premium passengers to their onward destination.

Paul had booked into a small boutique Hotel, in the trendy part of the City, The House.

He checked into his room and called his Australian contact Karin Moore.

"Hi, this is Karin, please leave a message and I will call you right back."

He dropped the receiver back on its cradle without speaking. 'Rules for life' he called them.

He tried twice more, and then gave up until the following day. Karin answered and they arranged to meet in the new Lemon Grove Brasserie, for lunch.

She recognised Paul from the Copenhagen meeting and they chatted about anything other than the reason for him being there. He found her attractive and liked her outgoing personality. He soon realized there was chemistry between them, but that was as far as it would go. Karin had another agenda but focused on the project and the matter of Mr Taqi Al-Wahid, and his 3 friends.

"Let's walk." She grabbed his arm as they strolled along the harbour edge. Laughing and teasing, but only for onlooker's benefit. Immersed in the theatrical display she outlined the ANP story, and the plans to widen the World's fear of Insha'Allah.

They agreed the plan, Markku impressed with her detail and background work. The talk moved on to her' insiders' with Taqi Al-Wahid. She sadly reported there had been no contact from the 'English girl, who Markku realized, without mentioning, was actually a fellow Australian.

The following evening Karin called Azil's mobile.

"Azil speaking who's that?"

"Karin."

"Hiya."

"Can we meet, same place, same time tomorrow."

"Yeah, all of us?"

"No, just you."

He read the message completely wrong, and spent the rest of the night fantasying over the fit looking young lady. A young lady who could kill him, with her bare hands.

By the harbour she met Azil, as Markku watched from a park bench, just like in the movies, except if anything went wrong, the luckless Azil would be dead within seconds.

He nodded and smiled a lot. She noticed he looked a little smarter in his dress style and knew her sexy deceit had drawn him in. He went to kiss her goodbye but she stepped away thrusting an extended arm towards him. He glumly shook hands, ego almost draining into the blue harbour swell.

Markku grinned from his bench warming duty.

"Come Cosmo." She started to jog away with her faithful guardian beside her. Azil watched her run, and felt the full undignified male pang of rejection in his stomach, and groin.

A mile away she relaxed and waited for Markku. "It's on. He will call the ANP and mimic Taqi. He will tell them they are planning a spectacular in Newcastle to emphasis the power they have, and to get the boys and their families out of town for the weekend. That should set the proverbial cat amongst the pigeons!"

"Excellent. I'm hungry, shall we grab lunch?"

"Not dressed like this, come back to my apartment and I will change, we can go to a new rooftop place in the centre, it's supposed to be 'awesome' as the yanks say.

They walked the panting dog back to her apartment. The impressive building housed 50 luxury apartments and the concierge welcomed her as Mrs Shelby.

Her apartment was the penthouse with stunning vistas over the famous Opera house and river. He sat on the terrace with a cold beer and soaked in the hot sun.

He could hear her in the shower; he walked inside for a top up. As he looked up she walked naked from the steaming room into her bedroom. He enjoyed the brief view of her muscular tanned body and emotions stirred,

He called out, "Is *the Mrs* part, of Mrs Shelby true." He was flirting.

"No, stops me getting pestered though."

"Yeah, I can imagine that might happen," he called loudly as she entered the room.

His eyes went to her immediately; she looked enticingly sexy in a small ribbed top and a flared short skirt. Hair hanging across her eyes in a sultry smouldering style.

" This do?"

His grin answered her question.

"Let's go." She patted her dog, "Cosmo be a good boy, look after Mummy's house."

They arrived at the packed new restaurant. They had no reservation but the maître'd took one look at Karin and fussed with this booking list, desperate to find her a table.

They enjoyed the afternoon and the food was extraordinarily good, 'Plates from around the World, Platinum style.'

Markku ordered the Belgian Mussel Bowl and fries, Trappister beer added authenticity, Karin not unsurprisingly selected a Greek Salad, with an Ouzo shot starter.

They both looked shocked when their two meals arrived, this was far from basic food and each carried bonus dishes similar to Spanish tapas bars. It was light and beautifully prepared. The couple looked like any other, deeply involved on their personal conversation.

Unlike others they were planning a spectacular, and the venue had changed in the last 2 hours.

Chapter 29

Newcastle, Australia.

Rossco Jedelavic had called an emergency meeting of the 15 man ANP following another call from Taqi Al-Wahid.

He called for order, strain etched on his purple face.

"Guys, I had a call from Taqi Al-Wahid this morning."

The audience leaned forward to a man. George Branson had already quit the group and left Newcastle in a hurry. Others were frightened at the prospects of further retribution from the Middle Eastern maniac.

"They have transferred half a million bucks to us, to show their commitment. They have also told me there will be an attack on our town this weekend and for us to make sure our families are not put in danger. I assume you gather what that means."

The floor erupted in pandemonium. Their resolve had gone. "No one wanted this when we started Rossco, it was a pipedream and kept us connected to the old days, this ain't right, attacks and the like."

Rossco held up his hands for silence but the aggression was fervent.

"I'm out" yelled a second voice.

"Me too." Another copycat.

The catcalls continued as Rossco lost control of the meeting.

"We gotta tell the cops, fuck this, it has gone too far. Rossco you have dropped us in the legendary dung, you need to get down town and explain this as one gigantic mistake. Look what happened to George's girl, marked for life."

The room vocals increased, feelings running high.

"OK, OK." Rossco banged his fist on the table. "I will talk to the coppers, just beware we can't stop this now, we are involved and there will be consequences from both the law, and the Arab."

"It's gotta be done Rossco. We have been foolish" The voice was calm and came from the back of the room. It was George Branson.

"George, we thought you had split."

"I did. But where do you hide, who are your friends. I would have spent the rest of my life wondering when I was gonna be caught, me and the family. It's over fellas, let's turn ourselves in and give the authorities chance to find this bastard. It's not just down to Rossco, we all gotta stand up and be counted."

"He's right." Echoed another voice from the group. As one they slowly walked to their battered Utes and drove in convoy of swirling dust, to Newcastle's main Police station.

At first the desk Sargent thought he had a group of practical jokers on his hands. The mention of Taqi Al-Wahid and the threat of an attack soon had him dialling Special Branch.

Chapter 30

Paris, France.

Coco and Ingrid settled into their First Class seats for the long flight to Japan and onwards to Okinawa.

"How was Michel last night, he seemed pretty upbeat at the restaurant."

Coco winced. "He made no sexual approach towards me, so I took control, ha. My Oscar is in the post. Didn't feel right, but it will pass. I love him dearly."

The service on JAL was exceptional and soon the talk turned to Ingrid's new man and the next move.

"Not sure." Her non-committal reply. "He is charming and yes he is sexy but I know so little about him. I even checked the Internet for background."

Coco mocked her. "I am shocked, has come to this nowadays, you date a man, then try and find out what he's like on the internet. Hardly romantic. You are adults, go for it. Pretend he is a sound engineer with a band or something." Reminding Ingrid of her relapse at the weekend.

Ingrid opened her newspaper and flicked through the pages. "Excitely she turned to Coco, "Look there's an article on Star Buck in Le Monde."

The pair read the copy together. "Hell Mr Free does not waste any time, the article reeks of his PR offensive."

"The review is very favourable," Ingrid remarked,

"Yeah probably to do with the journalist, finding a nice young female, knocking on his hotel door in New

York, late that evening."

"Ouch, you cynic." Ingrid bounced back at her.

"Actually she was good, looks like he has another winner on his books." Coco silently wondered how long before she succumbs to his charms. She shuddered at the memory of the lewd morning romp.

"Confident young thing. She said something really odd when I spoke to her at the After Party. She was completely wasted, but when I mentioned the Sapo Verde apartment she said had lived there for a few years."

Coco looked at her. "Odd."

"Odd, but she knew quite a bit about the layout, the car and so on".

"Yeah, but it has been featured in every magazine in the World, she is probably hoping Bjorn will set her up there." As she said it she felt a slight twinge of jealousy, ruffle her calm

Chapter 31

Sydney, Australia.

After the lunch they chose to walk back to her apartment block. They had agreed to change the spectacular target to the 'Platinum.'

"The impact will be greater, we can deal with the ANP later, if they

have n't already bottled it, and run for the hills."

His jibe closer to the truth than he realized.

They had booked for the following day as they left the skyline restaurant, the maître'd happy to salivate over the attractive Zoe Winner, for a second day running.

They were welcomed like old friends when they arrived the following evening, for their 8.00pm reservation. The enjoyed another meal but avoided any alcohol and called for the bill, before they had finished their main course, exaggerating a sudden illness for Markku.

They paid cash. It was cover for routine checks, which would be made on the guests list; it would be assumed the table for 2, booked by Zoe Winner and partner, had perished in the explosion. If, there were any such material readable, following the devastation caused by the liquid.

Markku attached the small box of ELG-9 to the underside of the table with industrial strength tape; it was easy to work, with his hands hidden by the crisp white linen table cloths.

She returned to her apartment to join Markku. Only after she had met and paid Azil and the 3 Moroccans, this time she had chosen a small unused lock up garage, close to the harbour wall.

Markku was already set up and she watched as he ran through the procedure on his laptop. He ended with an 8-digit code and from their window view; they watched the Platinum restaurant explode like a firework display.

"You might as well stay the night with me. I could do with letting off some excess energy." She walked away, not waiting for his response.

The seductive walk was too much for him.

He left in the morning, leaving her with 2 Mobiles and a brief 15-minute instruction on the activation process. His goodbye kiss was genuine affection and his mind danced with guilty thoughts. *Pleasure usually needs an alibi.*

Three days later 4 bodies were fished from Sydney harbour. There was no obvious evidence of the cause of death and the authorities, mindful of the forthcoming Olympics, did not want controversial publicity surrounding the deaths of 4 illegal immigrants.

The Moroccan Embassy collected the 4 bodies, and re-patriated them to their distraught families.

Chapter 32

Camden, London, England.

The samples freighted overnight from Nairobi worried Commander Jennifer Drew, head of forensic at Morrison House, Camden.

She had seen this before, almost 4 years ago after the Gatwick bombing. She recalled it was shortly after the discovery, that her capable assistant, Beni Al Wahad, was found dead in her St Johns Wood apartment. The Post Mortem examination never found the cause of death.

She turned the powerful overhead to maximum and dropped a small white pebble, onto the US Soldiers burnt uniform.

The colour of the white pebble made of compressed sulphur and three different oxides blossomed like a spring flower, turning the coat of the pebble grey.

"Shit." She looked up at the large IKEA clock. 2. 35am. "Shit." She repeated.

It was protocol and the rules are strict, it did not stop the humanitarian side of her worry about waking the Prime Minister at this hour.

She had taken a second call regarding another large bomb in Australia; the link indicated both bombings carried hallmarks of Insha'Allah.

For the first time in 4 years she punched in the 2-digit code for Downing Street.

It was answered on the first ring. "Go ahead." No preamble on the 'urgent matters only' dedicated line.

"Commander Drew, Morrison House. I have a code 5, which needs the Prime Ministers immediate attention. A well-rehearsed script.

"Understood Commander, Code 5, connecting you now. Stand by."

A series of pulse tones and then the voice of the Prime Minister wearily greeting her. "Commander."

"Prime Minister we have a serious matter concerning ELG-9 and the possibility that Insha'Allah are in procession of same."

"Right, understood. Number 10 as fast as you can. Will you advise the Commissioner?"

"Yes Sir." She short dialled Robert Dennis passing on the news from her mobile. She was racing down Park Lane at over 100mph within 5 minutes.

In Barnes a tired Timothy Jade, the PM's personal aide, was roused from his bed by a call from William Etherington and collected by 2 special branch officers, within 6 minutes of Jennifer Drew's call.

The assembled party of 4 were in situ within 20 minutes.

Commander Drew read the evidence and added news of the Australian bomb, which the others had yet to hear. The assessment of Insha'Allah involvement was hearsay, but they needed more information.

"Tim."

Timothy Jade sprinted from the kitchen where he was preparing coffee for the group. "Yes PM."

"Get me Robert Duncan, the Aussie PM. Secure line only."

"Sir."

Less than 30 seconds later the familiar accent of Robert "Bobby" Duncan came on the line.

"William, you must have heard."

"Yeah, is it bad?"

"Worse than bad William, top 2 floors of an 18 storey block, bomb went off in the new panoramic restaurant, fuck I ate there myself last Monday. Lot of collateral damage in the streets, no immediate claims, but we reckon the toll will hit north of a 1000 people."

"Bobby, we have reason to believe it could be ELG-9."

"Who the fuck are they?"

"No, that's a code for a liquid bomb. We had one here 4 years ago."

"Have you met Commander Jennifer Drew? Head of our forensic shop in Camden."

"Yeah, I believe so."

"I would like to send her to help you, she has knowledge of this type of bomb, and the really bad news is she has just checked the samples sent for the Kenyan bomb, that is confirmed as ELG-9."

"Oh bollocks, how bad is this stuff?"

"Nuclear plus."

"Fucking hell, send her over by DHL, we need her quick. We are looking into a situation in Newcastle where a local activist group were threatened by Taqi Al-Wahid himself. Not sure if they are complete nut bags but we have 15 of them in custody. They said there would be an attack in Newcastle so it could be a lead, or it could be more piss head bollocks, pardon my German."

"Bobby I will get Jenny on an RAF flight within the hour."

"Cheers William, send me the info and we will look after her."

Timothy Jade was already speaking to Northolt arranging for an emergency flight. A marked Police Range Rover pulled into Downing Street and Commander Drew was at the small airfield on the A40 inside 15 minutes.

Her plane was airborne before they coffee finally arrived on the PM's desk.

Chapter 33

London, England

Markku cleared the busy airport terminal with ease and joined the taxi rank he was fast becoming familiar with. He returned to the Lanesborough Hotel on Hyde Park, and fell into bed exhausted.

When was disturbed when his phone rang. He looked at the number but could not place it. He answered, "Hello."

"Trond is that you." He recognised the voice of Taqi Al-Wahid. "Yes."

"Trond we have been playing games."

"Fuck games, I could be banged up for 30 years you bastard."

"Yes, not a pleasant thought is it? Trond, I have some bad news for you, we uncovered a spy in our camp, a rather sexually aggressive young lady who we thought was English, but it appears is a country girl, sorry, an extremely wealthy country girl, from Perth, Australia. Regretfully she let slip her wealth, which alerted our internal security."

"I have no idea what you are talking about."

"No I suppose you would n't have would you. Just so as you don't think this is a bluff does the name Karin Moore mean anything to you?"

"No, who is she?"

"She as you call her, is her contact. We are looking for her now."

"Well good luck."

"Oh before you go, as you are in London," Markku froze, "a package has been left at Victoria Station, Box 1189.Opposite platform 9. The key is with the nice man who sells newspapers, just beside the row of boxes. Of course, if you don't know this woman, then it is of little interest to you. Consider it a present, one of my old Sorbonne colleagues has helped me out, nice chap, cut above the rest as the Brits say. Ha. See you."

The line closed and Markku pondered his options. He called Aaron and agreed to meet first thing in the morning.

Next he called Karin in Australia. "Hello."

"It's Paul."

"Hi Paul, miss you."

Karin, you are compromised. Move immediately, immediately understood.

"Yes, will follow Yellow."

"OK. Be careful."

Karin pulled her pre packed holdall from under her bed, the same bed she had enjoyed a deliriously sexual encounter with Paul Hush from England.

She walked through the row of expensive cars reaching her vintage '68 Porsche. She opened the door and reached under the front seat picking a small square box from its hiding place, she patted the Porsche, "See you later Porky."

Her eyes scanned the selection of cars; a wide choice in the luxury apartment's car lot, the new Rolls was attractive but too ostentatious for tonight's escape journey. A high end Holden caught her eye.

"Yeah she will do." She skipped alongside the driver's door and was inside the car instantly, a few fumbling seconds under the steering column and the engine fired. She eased the big car up the narrow car park ramp and towards the main road. She was out of the building and heading West within 4 minutes.

She checked for surveillance using the code 'Yellow' guide, something Markku had written during inactive times. She had been driving 30 minutes but was still only 4 miles from her apartment. She was now confident and headed West on the M4 Freeway, and her rescue point, a place called Hen and Chicken Bay.

Markku stayed awake all night, unable to figure how Taqi Al-Wahid knew he was in England, security breaches disturbed him, he was not a believer in co-incidence.

Aaron called at 7.00 am and told him to walk to the 'In and Out club' on Piccadilly, ask for Roger Ryman. "Be there for 8.30."

He left the hotel via the rear entrance and walked the entire circle of Hyde Park corner. The traffic was already busy. He walked into the Hilton hotel and took the express lift to the 32nd floor. The breakfast room offered a wonderful view of the Park, Park Lane and the Lanesborough front entrance. He pressed a £20 note into the head waiters palm and 'suggested' a seat by the south facing window.

The buffet offered a wide range but he filled his plate without concentration and walked back, juggling a machine coffee in his left hand. He stood drinking, starring out of the window, not an odd site for tourists, enjoying the bustle and beauty of England's capital city.

He was looking for unusual activity, either outside the main entrance, or across the road, hidden by two arches. It only took him a few minutes, the small Mazda car parked on double yellow lines had two occupants, the car was facing the hotel, but you would not see it if you exited the main doors, because when the first taxi broke from the rank, it would obscure any targets view. They had to be' watchers'.

He left the room and slipped into one of the 3 lifts, pressing car park as he did so. The lift lurched, frightening the two Arab children clinging to a woman in full Burka, just suspicious eyes visible.

In the car park he walked to the small pay booth where the sullen African attendant ignored him. It didn't help his demeanour and he quickly looked around for pedestrian traffic, or the sound of car engines starting.

It was too early. He whipped the door open and grabbed the burly man by the neck, a click echoed across the bare car park, rebounding off the walls. He remained still, easing the lifeless body to the ground inside the cramped hut. He selected three sets of keys from the small hooks and a spare yellow high visibility slip over. He started pointing them at cars hoping to ignite alarm flashers. The third area he pointed, there was success, a BMW 5 series flashed back 'hello'.

He swung into the seat, and smashed his way through the barriers, wood and metal flying in the air.

He raced out of the car park and turned back in front

of the hotel, left onto Park Lane and then right at Admiralty Arch. A flick of the steering and he was pulling up behind the small Mazda

He was sure, they were checking the hotel. He walked up behind them with his yellow vest on and knocked in the driver's window, startling the man.

"You can't park here mate." The passenger looked down at a crumpled A3 picture, it was of Markku. He flipped the small canister into the foot well and covering his mouth ran back to the BMW. The sudden steaming mist inside the Mazda sent two poorly trained observers to their maker, "or a few virgins" Markku mused to himself.

He abandoned the car in the NCP car park in Swallow Street and strolled round to meet Aaron for breakfast, "been a busy day so far," he said to his other self.

Aaron greeted him with a worried look. "This is getting difficult Trond."

"Yes I have just eliminated a couple of plums opposite the hotel, not sure where they picked me up but it could have been in Nairobi, he met me on his own and I imagine there were others there, I slipped up on this occasion."

"Let's get whatever is in Box 1189." Aaron had also considered their options and it was an impossible choice. "Could be a trap of course."

"I'll go on my own, do you want to stay here."

"Yes, no point blowing my cover as well."

Markku walked outside onto Piccadilly and crossed the road into Green Park. He walked 50 yards along the pathway, parallel to Piccadilly and exited back onto the road. He picked up no sign of surveillance. He flagged a taxi and asked for Victoria train station, "Can you wait for me, I will be 10 minutes and then I need to go back to the In and Out Club. "

"Sure Guv, but the clock is ticking all the time."

"I understand, he passed a £50 note through the hatch window."

"Hope this is real Guv," the cabbie joked.

Markku walked slowly through the busy hall and looked at comatose drunks and people sleeping rough. He carried on, finding the boxes and the newspaper stand beside.

He walked up to the news stand," I have been told to collect keys for Box 1189 from you."

"Have yer now. Here they are, geezer with the false beard said you would pay me £30. This ain't fucking Candid Camera is it?"

Markku had no idea what Candid Camera was, but handed over £30. He walked in the opposite direction of the Boxes.

"Oi, 'ere they are mate." Mr News was pointing at the boxes.

"It's OK, I will collect later.

"Fucking foreigners!" The newsman muttered.

Markku walked past a few victims of society, drunks he called them. A teenage kid was urinating against a wall, just 20 feet from a toilet.

He turned to see the disgust on the Scandinavians face.

"Don't give me that fucking look you arsehole, its 20 fucking pence to get in there." He pointed at the new toilet facility.

Markku was calm. "How would you like to earn £20, he waved a crisp note, showing the Queen's portrait.

"Yeah, maybe."

"See that row of boxes there?" He pointed at the line of postal drop boxes.

"Sure."

"This is the key to box 1189. All you have to do is run down there, open the box and bring me the package inside, and then you get the £20."

"Alright, sounds cool. What's in there drugs, or som'at?"

Markku had reached the end of his patience with the grubby youngster. He stepped onto his dirty bare feet and grabbed his balls in his strong right fist.

"Look arsehole, I am in a fucking hurry, if you have any thoughts of running off with the package I will find you, and snap your legs so bad you will be in a wheelchair for the rest of your life. Clear?"

The man's eyes were screwed in pain and tears were running down his cheeks. "Crystal, please mate, you're hurting me bad."

He released his savage grip and the youth limped towards the boxes, looking behind in fear, every 5 paces.

He walked back with a shoe box and they exchanged gifts.

"Thank you, that was n't so bad was it?"

The youth walked away," eager for a proper breakfast

for once. Three cans of Special Brew would set the day up perfect.

Markku returned to the waiting cab and was reunited with Aaron at the In and Out Club. They had a private room and looked at the box from all angles. "Looks harmless enough." Said Aaron.

Markku primed the side flap, eased the opposite side and tried to look inside without lifting the lid. "Oh fuck!"

"What!" a nervous cry from Aaron.

"Bloody stinks" He lifted the lid carefully and saw brown skin, decaying brown skin. Matted strands of hair clung to the skin.

There was a note.

In spider handwriting it read, "This box contains the skin of the Australian whore, you infiltrated into my inner circle. The rest of her can be found at Trodenhiem Avenue, Number 50. Flat 2. Copenhagen 14."

Aaron left the room to be sick.

He returned wiping his mouth. "What kind of animal does such a thing?"

"It's our World Aaron. I will go to Denmark and then pick up Karin; can you get Pieter Muller to deal with the other mess in Newcastle?"

"Yeah, he will like that."

"I know." Markku smiled, thinking back to some of the better days of latter years.

Chapter 34

Hen and Chicken Bay, Australia.

Karin eased the comfortable Holden along the smooth roads, until the Freeway gave way to a country road, not maintained to such a high level. She followed the 'yellow guide' to the letter, "you don't mess with your own life." Paul's endearing advice, ringing in her ears.

The journey took a long time, due to the constant need to 'park and view' the next 15 passing cars, every 5 miles, the same routine. At 25 miles she turned the car around and headed back towards Sydney, checking for copies, she drove 10 miles back and repeated the system. She noted no suspicious vehicles.

On the back, seat Cosmo grumbled.

She looked over the seat, tears in her eyes. She parked outside a closed transport café, huge lorries used the amusingly named, 'Piss Stop Café,' justification for the expansive parking area. She opened the rear door and Cosmo jumped free, small tail bobbing with pleasure.

She pressed the gun against his head and fired once, killing her best friend.

"Sorry mate, microchip technology makes you a liability." She lifted him towards the fast flowing brook, running alongside the café, and bundled the dead body into the cold water, hoping he would provide a meal, for any hungry stray animals. She breathed in hard, wiped the tears from her face and walked back to the Holden.

She stopped dead in her tracks. Beside the Holden was a Police Patrol car, the hard looking Officer, menacingly walking around her stolen car. He looked up and she could see his holster was unfastened. Her gun was in her left hand and pointing towards the floor. "Had he witnessed her shooting her own dog?"

'Chance is a difficult game. Don't play it'.

"Everything alright Miss?"

"Yes Officer, just caught short, sorry."

"You were travelling out here on your own?" He had his radio in his right hand, and casually flicked the stand by switch on.

Her reaction caught him unawares. He slumped to the ground without even touching his own gun; her single bullet had entered his head, directly between his eyes. The silencer had smothered the gun's signature.

She threw a mobile phone into the driver's seat and walked back to her car.

Karin finally reached the Bay and parked the Holden, removing the holdall, and her laptop bag. Her gun was tucked in her belt under a loose silk top, which billowed in the light breeze. She was looking for The Chicken Bay Café, it was 6.00pm.

The café was easy to find; it was the only café on the wide dusty road. A few old wooden buildings, poorly maintained and randomly scattered, gave the area a sad image. Small banks of grass and weed, defining the road.

It had the essence of a tourist site, one that never sees any tourists.

She slipped against the outside of a wooden building,

expertly crawling underneath the raised foundations. She had a clear view of the café and could see the owner fussing around the coffee machine, wiping table tops and the counter, glass encased tiers displayed cakes and sandwiches.

A woman with a small Jack Russell walked past and the dog picked up her scent, he barked aggressively until his owner snapped a command, his tail battered the early evening air, but he moved away in a happy mood.

The café lights dimmed to dark in a sequence, as the man shuffled around the room. He walked to the door and stepped into the cooling air, double locking the glass door. He limped away using a white stick to propel himself along the uneven dirt road. She rolled out of her hiding spot and crept silently towards the man.

He suddenly cocked his head to the side and half turning said "Good evening Miss Moore."

She stood rigid in the dust. "How the fuck did you know?" She then saw his white stick for the first time. "You're blind."

"I know."

"Sorry, I didn't mean that ..."

He stopped her, "Don't worry young lady; it's a gift I was given, after I lost my sight."

"You run a cafe and yet you are blind?"

"There you go again, I maybe blind but I am alive. When a beautiful young lady creeps up on me from behind, I can sense movement. I am even aware you have nice firm breasts and a figure to die for."

Karin's face lightened, but she did not comment.

"Oh, alright, the last fact is a personal fantasy; in my World I only have stunning, sexy customers." He rambled in his own humour.

"I could be ugly with a huge arse."

"So? Make no difference to me would it." He rolled his tongue out towards her, laughter lines covered by un-even 4-day stubble." Sorry, I was like you, 'in the field' before this," he pointed to his eyes. "I miss the madness of it all."

She felt a little sorry for him as his tone dampened. "How did you lose your sight?"

He smiled, "Over indulgence in masturbation when I was a teenager."

They both laughed together. It was Military humour, which she appreciated.

"I lost it in a freak accident. I was attacking a small building in Angola, just two of us, can't even remember who was paying us, but in those days it didn't really matter. We attacked through the rear and I launched my grenade into my target room, but Josh, my back up, went too soon and as I rushed forwards his aim exploded right in front of me. We got away, as you can see, but I spent 18 months in a hospital bed. Ended up here, courtesy of a few VIP contacts. You are my second 'job' in three years, so it must be high season out there. Ha"

She smiled and touched his hand.

"We walk this way; I will take you, and your laptop, to the pick-up point."

She didn't bother to ask how he knew she was carry-ing a laptop.

As they approached a large house set back on the road he spoke again.

"Don't worry if a huge dog charges from the big wooden fronted house, it is a daily ritual between us, nothing to fear."

She removed her gun to the front of her jeans.

"No problem, I love dogs" she felt the bitterness of Cosmo, much more than the wasted Police Officer's life.

She heard the growling menace of a large dog and looked toward the house. A huge muscular Rottweiler was charging down the slope, leading from the door. She touched her gun again.

"Don't." he said.

He knelt on one knee, holding his white stick like a staff, vertically beside him. The aggressive dog maintained his pace until he was just feet away, he slowed and edged towards the blind man. The two faces barely 6 inches apart. The dog's nose was perforating the air at intense speed; it glistened with small beads of sweat. The Blind man reached into his pocket and removed a small chicken leg. He placed it in his own mouth and the dog sat, drooling from loose jaws. He said 'whisper' to the powerful animal and he silently clamped his mouth. At the snap of the two sets of teeth colliding, the Blind man said "OK"

The Rottweiler gently removed the chicken leg from his mouth and scampered back towards the house, his legs dancing, canine pleasure from the 'theft.'

Karin smiled and helped him upright. "You do that every night?"

"Yeah, makes my day."

They reached the main lake and he pointed to an area on the opposite side. "Behind them trees is a narrow strip, enough for a light plane to land. Hide in the trees and he should arrive at 7.00am. He will wait less than 30 seconds, if you do not show, you are on your own. If *he* doesn't show, then repeat the same tomorrow." He passed her a small box from his bag.

"Here are some energy snacks, chocolate and some bread with 3 bottles of water. Good luck, it has been nice talking to you."

"Thanks. I don't know your name, you a Brit?"

"Names not important lass, and I am not a Brit, I am English." Adding another shot of humour, "from Barnsley, the sex capital of the North."

She grabbed his hand and placed it on her right breast. He smiled and gently squeezed her nipple. "How does that compare with your fantasy?" She joked.

"Not as big as some of my regulars, I'm afraid."

He 'watched' her walk away. "Hey, gimme a wiggle, sexy lady."

She obliged.

Karin was grateful for the drinks; the night seemed to stay forever. She said a prayer for her dog, and one for herself.

At 6.55am she heard a drone. She looked in the skies and picked out a small plane, silently descending towards the rough strip. As the plane bounced onto the soil she emerged from the thick undergrowth, and raced towards the swivelling machine.

The pilot was busy aligning himself for take-off; the

door flew open, a man, who looked like a cartoon farmer, bellowed. "Get in!"

She launched her bag into the cockpit but retained a safe, one handed grip, on the laptop.

"Good morning." The ruby faced man greeted her. "Where to?"

"You must be fucking joking! I have no idea."

He laughed, "Just me little joke. All under control ma'am."

The plane banked and she glanced at the wings, the interior was old fashioned and smelt musty. "What is this?" she asked

"Crop-duster, ma'am."

She looked at the wings and sighed. "Fuck me."

She flicked open her laptop and followed the sequence taught her by Paul Hush.

8 miles away a Police car exploded, damaging a few early truckers' wagons, in the process.

Chapter 35

Sydney, Australia.

Commander Drew eased herself from the nightmare 'comfort' of her RAF flight, touching down at Holdsworthy Airfield, in Sydney.

She was met by two Military Policemen who drove her at high speed to the Forensic laboratory, just a few miles away.

Lionel Beatty, the Chief Forensic Officer for the region met her in his cramped office, they had met previously at regular International Seminars.

"Jennifer, good to see you."

"Hi Lionel, wish it were under better circumstances." Her grim tone showing the stress she carried.

"What have we got?"

He pointed through a window at the end of the corridor. "We have at least 11 part bodies you could call them all NTB's."

"Right, so this was a bigger bomb then?"

"I am afraid so. News releases are talking of 875 but the real figure is closer to 2000, we still have 650 people unaccounted for, without accurate knowledge of ground floor collateral. It is bad Jenny."

"Let's get to work."

They changed into Lab uniforms and started their joint investigation. Jennifer had a small quantity of 'pebbles' but it was not long before she realized; this was indeed ELG-9.

"This looks like the biggest volume we have seen, bigger than the Kenya bomb."

"That was ELG-9 as well?" Lionel Beatty asked.

"Confidentially, yes Lionel, we need to agree to release this information as I fear there will be more attacks."

"What does this madman want?"

"We are not too sure. I need to get back to London. We have a worldwide epidemic on our hands."

Chapter 36

Adelaide, Australia.

Karin Moore stepped from the Crop-duster as it parked in a distant corner of the small wheat field. The nervous cartoon man, pointed at a car in the distance. She looked and could make out a white Toyota Land Cruiser with a single occupant.

She fingered her gun, releasing the safety.

Her heart skipped a beat as the large jeep speed towards her, driving the car was Paul Hush.

He beckoned her into the vehicle and she jumped into the open door and leaned over to kiss him, he pecked her cheek and said, "We need to move, pronto."

Paul gunned the vehicle down a small lane and veered off into a disused farmyard, he screwed the white jeep around the rear of a dilapidated barn and through a set of open double doors.

"Quick, change vehicles."

She obeyed the man they called the Magician, and raced him to the small black metallic Golf GTi. He was in second gear before her door closed.

"OK. Do you have battery left on that?" He pointed at her laptop.

"Just."

He handed her a list of sequence numbers and said "Go ahead blow that fucker up!"

They heard the muffled explosion in the distance as

the Golf raced along small roads towards the City.

They found an ordinary looking motel, and parked the fast car, making certain it was facing a clear exit route.

In the room in a low voice Paul walked Karin through the recent events with her 'insider.' Her name in their World was Barbara Guest.

She remained calm at the news, and the detail of boxed skin. Only when Paul revealed the horrific scene at the flat in Copenhagen did she flinch.

"When I found her, she was hanging from the shower head; she was skinned raw, every inch of skin Karin, every fucking inch. Blood had run down her body and her colour was like purple veins, she looked like an abstract painting. She must have been there 4 or 5 days; it is hard to imagine the pain she went through. But she was still alive. Barely. She was able to give me an address in Holland, she begged me for mercy."

Karin held her hands to her face. "Where is she now?"

"Karin I had no option, I had to shoot her, she was beyond death and in dreadful agony, it was merciful."

Karin walked away.

The pair sat silently for an hour.

Karin moved towards him and they embraced. She felt safe with him but knew they were still in danger.

"What did you do with her body?"

"I called the Arabic desk of an English newspaper in Wapping, London. Told them I knew where they could find the body of a young girl, whose only crime was to have fallen in love with married man. She had been subjected to a skin crucifixion, under the laws of Islam. I relayed them the story in Arabic."

"Why London?"

"The journalists there are more aggressive, they will add horrific agenda to the fact and the TV news will just run with their assessment. Before tonight ends, the whole of Europe will be running stories condemning Taqi Al-Wahid.

She made a shivering movement down her body. "Let's eat." She looked at her watch, "I have n't had a decent meal for two days."

"We can't go out. He called reception and asked if they could organize a take away Chinese, delivered to their room." Set meal for two will do."

30 minutes later the 'Cheng Chui Feast Meal for Two' arrived together with a complimentary litre bottle of Diet Coke.

The meal consumed, Karin looked towards him, her feelings changing as night beckoned. He read her thoughts.

"You sleep first, at 3.00am, I will wake you and you can stay vigilant until dawn, just in case."

"Shit." She breathed through tight lips. "Bloody protocol and rules."

She was asleep in minutes. Paul sat at the end of the bed and studied her calmed features. She didn't look like a highly trained killer, which made her all the more dangerous.

At 3.00am he gently rocked her. "Time for you to take over."

She stirred, "Sometimes this job sucks!"

"You do?"

"I certainly do."

He looked at his watch, as he placed his gun under the pillow.

"Ah, fuck protocol then, come here sexy."

She pushed him sideways and ran her lips towards his groin, she paused, "That blind guy was really helpful at the Bay."

"Sticky Finger Jack? He's not blind! Surely you didn't fall for that old trick?"

"Shut up, and think of wherever you come from!"

"You're already getting warm." He sounded a little frightened...

Chapter 37

Okinawa, Japan.

Coco and Ingrid were met by a smiling Rani Delaware. They swallowed him in a group hug and answered the usual banal flight questions.

"Mile High Club?" *It never happened.* Coco joked with herself.

They spent the day with Rani walking through the offices and various departments of Ashtimo. They discussed the hotel project and he was overly enthusiastic. "It sounds right on the money."

Coco winced. "He is sometimes, too American for me."

He had a car to take them to the Hotel Bacchus and promised to "collect them personally at 7.30pm for dinner at Toyo Towers." He begged, "Do not mention that when you see Mr Toyo!"

The day had been productive and the two friends sat in the lobby bar, waiting for Rani, a chilled glass of vintage Krug each.

Coco looked at her watch. "About time Jacque called." she teased.

"You know; you can be a real pain Miss Cicorre. I don't suppose Mr Free Love has bothered to call you?

"Oh. Below the belt, excuse the pun."

Their laughter a little too loud.

Two American businessmen eyed the pair, as if they

were buying a new Chevrolet. They walked over to the bar and perched on stools, a few feet from them.

"Hey Ladies, you in town on business."

Coco tap- touched Ingrid's knee. She blasted back at the two overweight men in thick French. Ingrid joined in with impossible Finnish. The two looked at each other and walked slowly back to their comfortable seats.

"What's Plan B, Jed?"

Rani entered the bar and escorted the pair past two open mouthed American's, all 3 of them chatting in perfect English.

Mr Toyo looked a little tired to Coco and she fussed around him asking after Nichito and Yuu, in particular his tennis career.

"He is doing really well on the circuit this season; I keep a look out for his progress. He must be due a Grand Slam soon?"

"Overdue," boasted Mr Toyo. "They may return to live in Japan, probably in Tokyo, he needs to be near an International airport."

The evening was delightful, the weather comfortably warm and they ate outside under an ornate Japanese pergola. Unobtrusive waiters added that private feel, so vivid in Japanese culture.

Nearing midnight Rani and Seonitno Toyo excused themselves, "To discuss a factory issue. We are sorry but we have a really difficult matter, it should not take too long."

Coco and Ingrid sat in the warm air; the pleasant relaxation was like a break after the weekends exertions.

The men had been inside over half an hour when Ingrid's mobile disturbed the serenity.

"Hi Jacque." Her face blushed as she avoided Coco's animated gestures. She walked to the bottom of the garden, waltzing in small circles as two new friends, accelerated toward a stronger, more meaningful relationship.

Coco smiled and turned away to give her friend the privacy these times demand. She wandered into the house, a waiter topped her glass without request and she found her son, and his retired boss, in deep conversation, pouring over charts and diagrams.

"What is so important you leave the two best looking women in Japan all alone for so long."

Mr Toyo looked shocked and paused his conversation. Rani placed a hand on his arm. "Sir, pay no attention, this is what the sad westerners call a wind- up."

"I see, most amusing Miss Cicorre."

She smiled turning on the French charm. Two men melted.

"What is the all this?" She waved her arms across the huge spread of paper.

The silence was broken by Mr Toyo. "Well as you can see, I still like to interfere with the big decisions at Ashtimo. We are developing a cure for various strains of flu, through our Pharmaceuticals Company."

Rani stepped back, looking at his mentor.

He continued "We have been developing a liquid, which can be produced in a variety of forms. As it is, the tablet option is less aggressive towards the symptoms, but the real challenge with the liquid dose is the size and the inherent refusal by the composition to run to an exact formula."

Coco wished she was back outside.

He rambled on, turning circles into squares, but then ended the monologue with the real issue.

"We know the liquid can cure many other bacteria, when it is 48 hours old it evaporates automatically, what you then see is likened to dry ice. However, there is no residue of any type, within the vessel the liquid was stored in. It cleanses 100%. Guaranteed each time"

"Coco engaged with her answer. "So if you can find a way to extract that dry ice moment you have a cure for many things, other than flu?"

"Yes, most likely. However, the evaporation is instant and the time can be calculated in seconds, capturing it at that moment is a stubborn problem. You kinda see it, and then you don't."

"How do you test this theory?"

Rani stepped forward. "This is confidential Coco and somewhat unpalatable to some Governments. We use live animals, mice, rats, dogs and even cats."

Coco did not waiver. "Go on."

"We have carried out tests on more than 1000 animals. The dosage is the issue. Too much and they would die, this is proven sad to say. Not hundreds but the first tests we a real disaster. When we lower the dose the animals are fine, we have this under a proper charted audit flow now. They are all tested at the end of the experiment, I don't really like the word as such, and they all rejected, or fought off the bacteria we gave them. The forced measures were by a variety of different methods, but the endgame results were a health indication of 94%. This is unnaturally high. The usual percentage average for this range of animals is 68%.

"Impressive."

"Sorry about that." They all turned to see Ingrid smiling like a schoolgirl in the glass doorway.

"Time we took these girls home Rani." Mr Toyo flapped his arms. "I hope we didn't bore you Coco?"

"Not at all. Good luck with the liquid. What is it called?"

"The product code is ELG."

"In the car Coco asked him about the test results. "Do you test them before you start the programme?"

"Yes. I assume so, but I will check tomorrow."

"That data might produce some interesting facts, those that had poor percentages before verses their results afterwards? If the average is so astronomically high, you must have cured some pretty powerful bacteria in the process surely?"

"It is on my TTD."

"You're what."

"Sorry, college jargon, things to do!"

As Coco undressed her mobile rang.

"Hello."

"Miss Cicorre." The formal voice of Seonitno Toyo. "Could we meet before you return to France? Just us two."

"Of course."

"Good, I will call you in the morning, good night and sorry to have disturbed you."

She held the handset, as if expecting it to speak to her.

Her tiredness had evaporated with the call, setting her fertile mind roaming. She walked to her balcony and flicked the switch to the Hot Tub. Foaming bubbles and deeply scented aroma filled the cool midnight air.

The mood lighting, helped compose an erotic atmosphere.

She took a small bottle of red wine from the mini bar and poured the contents into a highball glass.

Her clothes lay discarded on the private terrace.

"Shall I? Shall I?" Her mind, playing cruel emotion with her. She picked her phone from the table beside the tub and called Bjorn's private mobile.

"Hej, hej," The Scandinavian accent instantly exciting her.

"Hi Bjorn. Coco." She purred in her sexiest French tease. "I am in Japan, sitting naked in a hot tub, on a serenely private, perfumed terrace. My nipples are hard and I am thinking of you."

"Oh, just a minute Coco, it is Sven, Bjorn's chauffeur, I will hand him to you now."

Her expletive drowned, as she ducked under foaming water...

Chapter 38

Amsterdam, Holland.

Markku retained the same Paul Hush ID for the trip to Holland; the danger threat to Karin meant she took on the ID of her recently murdered insider, Barbara Guest. It was a risk but waiting another 24 hours for ID was a day lost. Pieter Muller had found the Passport at the flat in Copenhagen.

They strolled through the narrow streets of Amsterdam, anonymous amongst the stag and hen parties and large groups of overweight men, fresh from a night crawling the famous red light area.

He pecked her cheek on a regular basis, not for any ulterior motive or effect; he was beginning to gel with the tough girl.

They found the address, a 5 story terrace building, which must have been a stunning house in years past. Markku pointed at the other buildings and looked at the tourist map, holding it towards Karin.

He covered his face from view and said "The pink building looks a possible."

She spun round and grabbed his arm towards the opposite direction. They circled the block and came back to the front of the pink building, without any fear of surveillance detection.

The pink building looked to be unoccupied, the brass nameplate was badly marked and she read the name as ink Shirt Co."

"I think you will find that is the Pink Shirt Company."
He grinned at her mistake.

"It says Ink?" She argued,

"Yes it does but the typed note there," He pointed at
the door. "Is a real clue."

On the door a year-old sheet advised people The Pink
Shirt Co had relocated to 77, Beergen Strasse.

"I hate smart arses!"

"I love your arse." He patted the back of her jeans.

Ten minutes later they forced the rear door and entered the building. A few remnants of the previous landlord scattered across the floors. Together they explored
the higher levels. Both had their guns tucked closely
against their hips.

The building was empty, with no signs of squatters,
or cleaning company activity. They settled by the window
and could see directly into the target building opposite.

The day passed with little activity, either in or out. It
was clear that the building was occupied, mostly by Arabs,
or Asian looking people.

Markku encouraged "Look through the dress code, it
may be a disguise."

They had limited equipment with them and had to re-
ly on visual and memory for data. At close to midnight the
activity picked up and Karin gasped as she recognised her
Lebanese 'insider.' She was being herded inside the building with another 4 attractive young females.

"That's Yaheem."
Markku acknowledged and tried to track the girl's

progress through the floors of the building. "Front window 4th floor."

"Got her."

The pair watched as the girls, including Yaheem, were pushed into a room, without the shutters closed; the lights gave a perfect TV quality view.

Suddenly they saw him; Taqi Al-Wahid walked into the same room and strolled up the line of attractive females, like a military General reviewing his troops. He touched the girl's breasts, ran hands over their bodies and lifted the clothing of those in Burka robes.

He pointed at three of the five, which included Yaheem; the odd two were ushered from the room. The chosen group were led away and eye contact broken.

"They must have gone to the back rooms." Markku calmly made his assessment.

Karin was angry, but remained professional. "Look room to the left, 2nd floor."

The unwanted girls were being bundled into a room with a double bed, followed in by 4 men in robes. They systematically beat the girls, slapping and from the distanced view, appearing to spit on them. They continued their assault and then began to rake the clothes from the women. Within minutes a gruesome orgy was screened in the window light, the four men taking it in turns to rape the girls. Occasionally the girls were slapped, for no visible reason, other than power and control.

Karin's face showed her anger. "I can't watch anymore."

They stepped into a room at the rear of the building

and sat on the floor. They silently devoured the meagre food they had purchased for the night's watch.

"Animals." She snuggled against Markku and his warmth eased her tension. "She is in danger Paul; we need to get her out."

"Danger comes with the commitment."

"I know; it is more that we should ask of a woman."

"We need a plan. You try and sleep; it has been a hell of a week."

She lay on the cold floor but exhaustion soon claimed her eyes. She slept through until dawn, Markku watch her nerves jerking her body. Her unconscious reaction the tricks of sleep deprivation.

At 7.00am she stirred. "I will go and find breakfast. Stay alert." He kissed her. More tenderly than before.

She crawled towards the window and saw Yaheem staring straight towards her from the opposite side of the road.

Eyes locked, but both of the experts showed no reaction

Yaheem held her knuckles to her chin, rubbing her skin with her clenched fist, she extended five fingers rubbing her face with an upward action, she did this twice more.

Karin accepted the message flagging her hand in a downwards motion, meaning 'call over'

Karin was excited, but when she heard the sound of door movement she reached for her firearm and flattened herself against the side wall, out of sight from the rooms opposite.

She controlled her breathing, by increasing the rhythm. She waited and picked out a double set of footfall. She remained in position, 3 minutes ticked by. An audible whisper outside the door had her adrenalin bursting through her body.

The two men entered the room. From her vantage point she could see they were of Somali decent, both tall and dressed the same. White eyes stood proud against their smooth brown skin.

She moved from her shadowy hiding place. "Stand still." No aggressive command, but clear and crisp, she remained relaxed.

The 2 men laughed at her, her limited clothing hid the bulbous silenced gun. "And what you going to do, whore."

The man's forehead was shiny with sweat; she knew he was untrained in combat. She had the advantage point.

"The first one of you to look round dies, I am not alone and there is a gun trained on you." She pointed behind them with her empty hand.

The man on the left muttered something she could n't understand. He laughed and began to loosen his belt.

The other man joined the banter. "There's no one here girl, look." He turned away, looking behind him. The thud of the bullet entered his head just above the right eye. Blood sprayed the corner of the room. He dropped beside the second man.

Karin's gun was parallel to her waist and she shot his colleague in the groin, he screamed and a large knife fell to the floor. A second shot rang out and the man was silenced.

Markku stepped from the doorway clutching a plastic shopping bag.

"You need to sharpen up your shooting technique."

"I was aiming for his balls, he deserved a bit of pain. Guess his options of shagging 70 virgins are slightly reduced."

Markku kicked both bodies. "Coffee and croissants with cheese."

"Yuk. No fries?"

They ate the breakfast and she told him of the incident across the road.

"So 15 men."

"Maybe 13 now." She laughed.

"OK, we gotta move."

They packed their few possessions and escaped from the building. "We need a change of clothes."

"I'm up for that, ain't been shopping for a while."

Chapter 39

Okinawa, Japan.

Coco lifted the ivory telephone in her lounge. "Yes"

"Miss Cicorre, I tried your mobile but it doesn't appear to be working?"

"I dropped it in the bath Mr Toyo, too much of your fine wine I think."

His smiled radiated down the phone line. "Cover it in rice and heat in a microwave for 4 minutes."

"Does that work?"

"No but the explosion is quite fun." His giggle at odds with his age. "I will get my audio division to send round a replacement, one of our prototypes, probably reach the European market in 3 years, so you have a bit of what you call 'bing' I believe?"

"Bling"

"Ah so." He joked. "Shall I come to your hotel, say an hour."

"That will be fine. Suite 14."

She replaced the phone and wondered what the meeting was about. She

recalled the attempted phone sex with Bjorn, late last night. Frustratingly

ended by her embarrassed 'dive' under water.

She could not remove her growing feelings for the Rock boss.

The promised new Mobile arrived before Mr Toyo.

The polite Japanese engineer, Mito, transferred her contacts and settings to the new highly stylish Accental Mobile. The features were unbelievable and included many prototype concepts, including live Wi-Fi TV and some, not yet ready in Europe, scanner uses.

"If you have any issues with the local networks when you get home, call me and we can fix on line." Mito handed her a list of contacts and names within the Ashtimo FPU, Forward Projects Unit.

"You must have a very interesting job Mito."
"Yes I do, and we have a fantastic new boss, Mr Delaware."

Her pride was contained to a smile.

The door knocked again and Mito bowed as Mr Toyo entered. He spent time chatting to the young employee, no doubt making his day.

Seonitno Toyo accepted her offer of coffee.

"Miss Cicorre, it is so nice to see you happy and prospering so well. How is it working out with your son, Rani?"

"It is sometimes difficult but then life has its own index, and we have to try and fit in. It was a mistake, for me to consider it a right to appear 20 years late, and try and claim someone's life. I am grateful to you for the advice and I feel happy with the relationship. Mind you, I sometimes have a great urge to sweep him onto my arms for a motherly cuddle."

He nodded an understanding parental gesture. "Are you aware he has split up with his friend?" Unable to quite come to terms with 'boyfriend' as a terminology between men.

"Oh, no. He never mentioned it."

"He seems OK, but I thought you had better know."

"Is that why you wanted to see me?"

"No I could have told you this over the phone." They both laughed at the forlorn Blackberry sitting on the table. Her new Accental looked like it came from Outer Space, in terms of design.

He closed his hands in front of his stomach. "Miss Cicorre, you have developed Sapo Verde into a fantastic company, I read about you all the time, record profits, high customer satisfaction awards, wonderful new ideas, it never stops."

She blushed a little. "Thank you, I have a great team."

"Ha, you sound like a General speaking." His self-mocking joke adding to the bond developing between them. "I have an idea for you."

She rolled her eyes.

"I am sure you contribute greatly to Charity, but why not start one of your own, something personal to you."

"Go on."

"Simon Boaden was the reason you are here today, he was the originator of this business idea, which, first Melanie Preston stole and then you developed, with a little help from your friends?" He winked.

Coco was always edgy, whenever Melanie Preston's name surfaced. "You are right, and as much as I hate to admit it Miss Preston did an excellent job. It doesn't take away the pain of her part in Simon's downfall." She fingered her eyes, fighting away the tears.

"Everything in life, is not always as it looks Miss Cicorre. These are wise words."

She sniffed the air and walked to the kitchen area, bringing back a bottle of still water.

He continued. "I would be correct in assuming you have a considerable number of wealthy friends, and clients."

"Yes." She agreed.

My suggestion to you," He stopped. "I must call you Coco, the Cicorre word is hard to pronounce."

"At last." she thought.

"Find a cause that you have some personal relationship with, cancer, children with terminal illness, animals. Whatever it is must be close to your heart. Closer, than anything else. Once you establish conclusive belief, set up a Charity, call it The Simon Boaden Foundation."

Coco did not move. She bit her lip and swallowed trying to stop the emotional river building from within.

"Mr Toyo, that is the most wonderful idea I have ever heard." The tears were flowing and she could do nothing to stop them.

"Then it is done?"

"Oh. Yes, yes, yes." She flung her arms around him and he felt the damp tears from her face, roll onto his.

"This makes me happy also." He removed two envelopes from his pocket; these are your first contributions to The Simon Boaden Foundation. One from me, and one from your son."

The words, "from your son." Mean such a lot to me, thank you."

She opened the envelopes and gasped. There were two Bank Drafts for a million Euro's each.

"It's just the beginning Coco. Let's keep in touch."

"I promise. Thank you."

He closed the door and walked away, a happy elderly General.

Coco reached for her new phone. Dialled Ingrid's room.

"Get in here, quick!"

Chapter 40

Downing St, London, England.

"Good evening Commander."

"Hello Tim, not quite sure if it is evening, or morning, Wednesday, or bloody Friday actually.

"Ha, long day trip?"

"You could say."

He took her coat and noticed she was in the same clothes as two days previously.

"Commander we keep spare clothes upstairs, if you wish to change."

"Very kind Timothy, but this won't take long and I live 15 minutes away, 8 is my record actually."

He returned her smile, knowing her reputation as a competent 'blues user,' not always when on duty, or a call.

"Everyone else here?"

"Just waiting for late Rupert." A jibe at one of the COBRA group, who was always late. The phone from the 'Gates' bleeped."

Rupert Willis on site Timothy."

"Thank you" He looked at his watch and clenched his fist in the air." £20 to me tonight."

The staff held a small betting ring on matters such a lateness, same old suit, her jacket is too small, All manner of Political unkindness. Tonight Tim was the winner.

The assembled COBRA team thanked Jennifer Drew through the Chair.

She started her report. "I can be brief gentlemen, er and Ladies, apologising to the Home Secretary. The two recent bombings are confirmed to have been carried out using ELG-9. The first time this has occurred since the Gatwick bomb, when we reprimanded the Israelis. The concern here, and it is top level, both bombs have been accredited to the Insha'Allah organization although they have condemned this as Political influence, and deny any involvement. Which, given nearly 3000 people are likely to have perished in the two explosions, is probably understandable."

"Commander, are you aware of the further incident in Denmark, the skin crucifixion, as the red tops are describing it."

"Yes I was briefed on the way by The Commissioner. Awful, simply awful."

The PM tapped the table. "This could be detrimental to all the good work we have down in race relations in this Country, and around Europe for that matter. It does bother me that these acts are so horrific with no demands, or statements, toward reason. My conclusion, and this is all it is at present, is that this may not be Insha'Allah, it maybe someone wishing to pass blame on them, for their own hidden motives."

"Prime Minister that is not my field. I have this limited report and even more limited sleep. Do you mind if I retire from the meeting, and catch up with my body clock?"

"No, not at all. Thank you, Commander."

"One last point, which needs your decision, no other country is aware of ELG-9, and the devastation it can cause. We have the knowledge, but if we fail to pass this on we could find some allies turning against us. My emails are jammed with demands for information; it appears to have reached the press. Goodnight everyone."

Chapter 41

Henko, Finland

Star was pouring over her Press cuttings. She could recite them from memory, having studied the same ones for almost 2 weeks.

Anita's long phone call, had worried Melanie for over a week, and she was desperate to discuss it with Markku. That option was a closed door and she understood why. She had no idea their relationship was threatened by a sexy Australian girl named Karin Moore.

In just over a week she had agreed to meet Bjorn, in Paris for the contract signing. Almost for her to officially sign over her 17-year-old daughter, into the hands of the notorious Wildman of Rock. It was another curved ball in her life, but not the real burning issue, which she could not contain anymore.

Star had mentioned names such as Coco and Ingrid, how fab and cool they were. It was not a statement of substance, everyone she met in 'the business' was fab and cool. The thought of her daughter finding out her parental background was not, the sweet and caring people she envisaged, could lead to all sorts of emotional complications. Worse, she would find out her real Father was a corrupt villain, who killed people over a 100 peseta unpaid bet.

She lay awake at night, sweating from anxiety, and the lies she may need to conjure, to protect her identity, or ruin her talented young daughters' life. She craved rough sex at times like this, but, in his absence, had to content herself with DIY aids.

It came to her early one morning, as she sat in the lounge watching the dawn dance of light between the tall trees.

"I have to come clean, and face the situation."

There was one important person, she desperately needed to talk to, but she was unapproachable, in the extreme.

She needed a gamblers throw.

Chapter 42

Paris, France

Coco had talked through the Foundation idea and was a little upset when Michel, using his Lawyers hat, touched on the notion that there could be tax advantages for the Company.

Her resolve was severely tested when Suresh had the same response to the news.

Her explosive rant had the desired effect and no one mentioned any benefits again.

She had sketched a short list on the plane home with Ingrid, who was staying at her house preparing her schedules for her new role. Coco asked her to invite Jacque to dinner so as they could all meet. It was fixed for the following weekend, during one of many evening phone calls between the new pair.

Bjorn had not called since her phone dunking experiment, she worried he may be felt she was avoiding him, because of the embarrassing comments; she inadvertently made to Sven, his driver. She took the angry frog approach and picked up the phone. This time checking if he actually was the person answering his 'private phone'

"Is that tonight's sex line caller."

"Bjorn, I am so sorry about the other evening." She went through the whole scenario and they laughed together, laughed in an easy way, which teased her making her body tingle, and the hairs on her arm stand proud.

"Are we meeting next Monday, Anita has us down for 1.00pm at the George V. Will you be on your own?"

The weight of the question hung in the air. She paused, knowing the answer should be common sense, with a man like him. Instead she heard herself saying, "Of course." In a slightly overdone smouldering voice.

"See you there, can't wait." He sounded so different to the madness, which normally surrounds him.

"Oh Christ" she moaned. "I might as well have said get a room and become a real tart."

Michel's voice behind her made her jump. "What darling?"

"Nothing, just thinking out loud."

He walked away and she felt the numbness again. He had not approached her in a loving way since her return from New York, and always she made the moves. She was angry, and a little frustrated.

She walked into the garden clutching her prized new mobile, turning circles, like Ingrid does when talking to Jacque. "I have to find out." She said to herself.

She re dialled his number. He answered immediately. "Bjorn it's me."

"I know; your name comes up." He teased.

"Bjorn. Are you staying at the hotel Monday?

"No we are leaving for London that evening, taking Star to Abbey Road studios to cut her first hit."

His positive words a prompt to her confidence.

"Book a room for us Monday afternoon, don't tell anyone and don't ask me why, I must be mad."

"Yes Ma'am. I look forward to it."

Chapter 43

Amsterdam, Holland.

The surveillance of the Insha'Allah building had been compromised with the intruders. They were not sure if they had been spotted, or victims of a couple of chancers, out to rob someone. On reflection they agreed the latter was the most likely and as they could n't find an alternative, they headed back to the Pink building.

They split up and circled the block in opposite directions, No obvious signs. At the rear, there was no indication of further intrusion; they made their way through the floors, stealth their secret.

They reached the 4th floor; the two lifeless bodies were in the same position as they had left them. They dragged them down one flight of stairs and shut them in an unlocked room." At least we don't have to look at them." Karin said.

Again the daytime activities were slow, towards evening it increased and around 9. 00 pm the real bustle began, as more visitors came and went.

Shortly after 10.00pm a large people carrier pulled up. On this occasion 8 young females clambered from the car and were hustled inside by the men in robes.

"She's there. Yaheem." She said softly.

"OK. Got her."

They watched the same routine as the line of attractive girls were paraded in front of Taqi Al-Wahid. He groped breasts and buttocks and lifted the private world of the Burka, without any feelings. His first selection was Yaheem.

Karin saw the pain on her face but knew she would cope. He picked 4 girls and the rest went downstairs.

The same unpleasant treatment of the lower room was displayed, beatings and ugly violent abuse of the girls, the fear and loathing evident from their viewing gallery opposite the carnal lust. It was a vile and distasteful scene, which left the audience of two shaking their heads.

Karin touched his arm as Yaheem ran to the window, she tapped 2 on her wrist meaning she had less that 2 minutes. She turned her back moving an arm across, "round the back" read Karin. The Lebanese girl flicked fingers upwards either side of her head, "Wait and listen." She then crossed her arms across her breast which read "sleep." Four fingers, on her left hand, "at 4.00am" Finger to eye, "I." She jerked her fingers in a walking movement. "Go."

She sliced her hands, "Terminated". They saw her clear the room, back to the orgy room with Taqi Al-Wahid.

They read through her message again, trying to confirm was difficult because it happened so quickly. "We have no option." Markku making the decision. "We will need a car."

He waited until 3.00am and slipped out the back entrance. At the foot of the small slope her saw a Ford Transit van. He checked the car and decided this would do, the engine was cold and so unlikely just a drop off car, or some randy tradesman nipping into a girls flat for a quickie.

He walked around the rear of the target house, just to re assure himself. He noticed another vehicle, a Mercedes estate, old but big, His mind was made up. He opened the door and pulled the wiring down, but left it dangling. He silently laid the rear seats flat. He searched for something heavy and found a large slab of concrete, which he rested against the passenger door of the Ford.

He re-entered the Pink building.

He tried to surprise Karin but she was too good, and cuffed him from behind as he walked in.

"Ten out of Ten." He mimed with his thumbs.

He looked at his watch, 20 minutes to go. At 10 minutes to 4 they moved their bags to the ground floor. 5 minutes to 4 they walked to the Transit, Karin was in and had the engine running by the time Markku reached the passenger door. He had the heavy concrete on his lap.

They pulled the transit round the rear of the target house, letting the car coast in neutral with no engine for the last 40 yards. "Swing it around so the front is facing the rear entrance."

Karin did what he said without question. Protocol.

They opened the transit doors and walked to the back door of the house; they listened but heard no sound. Markku looked around hoping it was not a trap.

A shrill, accented female voice suddenly pierced the air. It was a firm, but calm, instruction, "Now. Push."

They both leaned on the door and it cracked and split like balsa. Markku could see the cross panels had been removed leaving pale patches where the fitting had been attached. Yaheem must have been preparing her escape for days.

She rushed toward them. "Turn left, silver Merc." She ran, the obedience instant.

There was movement inside the house as Markku re fired the transit engine, he revved the engine to maximum and waited for the first man to exit the doorway, He dropped the heavy concrete onto the accelerator and jumped from the van as it crashed its way toward the door. The first man took the hit square on and the transits height took the frame, bringing it down on the still racing engine, the doorway effectively blocked.

He turned and saw the headlamps were alight on the Mercedes and Karin had the tailgate open. He raced for the car as she drove away gathering pace. He lunged for the rear compartment and yelled "Safe!" She braked hard and the tailgate slammed with the motion, her right foot floored the throttle and the huge car swerved and snaked until she regained control.

"Who the fuck is this" asked the stunning Yaheem, face sweating, but eyes smiling. She ruffled her long hair, after gleefully throwing her headscarf out of the open window.

They drove from the City centre, obeying the traffic signals, but all three watching for signs of a chase. They stopped in a small suburban street and Karin selected a new car, for the onward journey. An anonymous, blue Skoda saloon.

They headed north on the A7. As dawn brought more traffic they entered Heerenveen and parked the car. They walked three blocks before finding a small café, just opening for the breakfast trade.

They ordered hot breakfasts and discussed their next move. Yaheem had an enormous amount of information, stored in her head, addresses, names, vivid descriptions of the lack of order within the Insha'Allah ranks.

"I need to talk up." Markku stood, both girls understanding the phrase. "Be 5 minutes." He walked outside the café and called Aaron, breaking normal field rules.

He briefly explained their situation, asking "Do we have anywhere safe in Holland."

Aaron's reply a sharp, "No. Can you get to Hamburg?"

"Yes, probably later today."

"OK, I will make the arrangements." The line died.

Markku returned to the café. Breakfast was waiting, "With two very attractive females, the day might just be fun, for a change he relaxed confident they were safe. For now.

Chapter 44

London, England.

The British tabloids were running riot with the skin crucifixion stories, the Television News channels had live coverage from outside the apartment in Copenhagen. Neighbours were given their 15 minutes of 'Andy Warhol' time, the usual so shocked routine, and nice comments about someone, they never knew.

Timothy Jade had the morning editions prepared on the PM's desk, as he briskly walked into his Downing Street office.

"Morning Timothy!" His usual rallying morning call.

"Good Moaning PM." He mimicked the 'ello 'ello TV signature phrase.

"And you may be right; the bloody hacks are in moaning overdrive I assume."

"Indeed they are Prime Minister, worse still, Spurs lost again."

"Send my application Tim, they will sack that chap by tonight." He joked as he lifted the Sun newspaper in the air. "Have they gone fucking mad?" His expletive changing the mood instantly.

"Thought that might rub you the wrong way, Sir."

The headline read STREETS OF FEAR and carried a photograph of a deserted Oxford Street, the busiest shopping street in Europe. The fear factoring ran for 5 pages, with expert opinion adding to the worried women all over

Britain. Exaggerated guessing claims - "there could be up to 20 more girls skin crucified, our sources in Denmark tell us."

"Sources in Denmark my arse, the only source the Sun have in effing Denmark is Tomato and bloody HP!" William Etherington was livid.

"PMQ's could be a bit spicy today sir."

"Should n't joke about it Tim. He flicked the pages "Wow, Candice from Mansfield looks a healthy girl."

"Absolute cracker, Sir. Favourite food is a bacon sandwich apparently."

"With, or without sauce Timothy?" He continued to stare at the big breasted, Candice from Mansfield.

Chapter 45

Hamburg, Germany.

They had left the stolen Skoda in Heerenveen and Markku had rented a high specification Opel, moving up the price ladder, until they had a car available with Satnav.

The call from Aaron had directed them to a house address in the North of the City. The female voiceover told them they were 'at their destination.'

The house was a suburbia classic, well maintained externally, neatly trimmed grass and a 10 year old Volvo estate in the drive. It looked perfectly normal.

There were obvious signs of life in the house, several rooms lit with the yellow glow of subdued lighting.

Markku rang the doorbell. The two girls stood 20 feet apart, Yaheem now discreetly holding Markku's gun. The door opened, a young man in his early thirties, beckoned them in quickly.

Inside the house was packed with old fashioned furniture, every space was occupied, the walls were covered in black and white photos and poorly framed drawings, by someone with little artistic sympathy, or talent.

The young man introduced himself as Jens; Markku did not bother with any introductions. "I am a Medical student, they asked me to check the girl is OK?"

Yaheem walked forward, his eyes lit up.

"Hello, please come." He motioned to the stairs.

"I'll come with you." Karin, acting the motherly role.

Markku wandered into the kitchen. Jens had laid out plates of cold food, sandwiches, rolls, rye bread, cheeses, sausages and ham. He boiled a kettle and searched for the coffee jar.

He was enjoying his snack when the 3 returned from the examination.

Yaheem was fine, a few cuts and bruises, but good readings from her vital stats. "She needs to see a proper doctor to check in more detail, but for now she is fine to rest here and wait." He nodded to the group and bid them farewell. Someone will come to collect her tomorrow; you will probably be aware who this is?"

Markku nodded. "Thanks."

Yaheem went to bed, leaving Markku and Karin alone in the eccentric, overcrowded lounge.

"Have you noticed something odd?" She baited.

"No, What."

"There is no TV!"

He smiled, "Then we had better find other ways of enjoying our evening."

Their lovemaking was long and tender; they romped on the springy sofas and laughed at each other's favourite stories, in-between the frequent sexual pleasure. The conversation headed towards each of their private lives, which is usually a no go area, protocol had long since been broken between the pair, and both opened their lives.

They quietly slipped into a bedroom and fell asleep, a bonded couple, now as one.

At midday Aaron Milan arrived and Yaheem left with

him for London to debrief. Aaron had provided a new set of ID.

The girls had already been into the City centre and bought her new clothes, trendy tops and uniform jeans. Her beauty enriched by the clothes, her personality altered, by the same magnification of the style swap.

Markku and Karin were ordered back to Amsterdam to continue their monitoring of Taqi Al-Wahid.

Both were pleased with the 'posting.'

They left the house mid-afternoon and headed back towards Amsterdam, they stopped for the night in Hoorn, finding a luxury 5 Star Hotel in the town centre, The Radisson.

Together they strolled around the small shops, mostly closed, but the odd few offering tourists a welcome. They found a Pizza restaurant and chatted over Pizza and beers.

As he paid the bill Markku casually whispered "Fancy a long bath and an early night, sexy."

"Yeah, who with?"

"You're going to pay for that young lady."

"Talk is cheap." She ran ahead of him towards the Hotel.

In the morning they reached Amsterdam in the Opel and Markku decided to return it to the Europacar office.

They booked into the nearest Hotel they could find to the Insha'Allah target House. It was a drop in luxury they both accepted.

Re positioned in the pink house they watched as the evening's ritual developed. The same bedraggled group of females arrived and the show was a repeat of the other evenings. The beatings and vile sex acts disgusted them more this time. Their conversations with Yaheem had revealed many more serious abuses in the basement rooms, which were out of sight from their high perched view. Girls were never seen again, she confirmed the skin crucifixion was a regular sentence, for any girl brave enough to say no to sex, with any male in the building. The danger of multiple unprotected sexual partners was ignored by the grubby men of religious obsession, they made their own rules or excuses, whichever suited the question.

"Hmnn, nice car." Karin looked down on the svelte lines of a black Porsche.

Markku looked over her shoulder. "Not my style." He said with a straight face.

"You are just jealous. I have a Porky in OZ. Not brand new like that, mines authentic, old, hard to drive and really aggressive. Bit like you. He, he."

"French plates." He looked closer at the car, jotting the registration on his hand.

The well-dressed man entered the building, but could not be followed inside from the open view they commanded, not until the orgy room had quietened down the miserable grubby men left. The girls were still in the room when the smartly dressed Porsche man entered. He took the arm of one of the girls and went out of the room. The other girls held each other clearly crying, concern for their friends' fate.

"Can you try and get a photo when he comes out?"

"Yeah, I would rather shoot the bastard." She replied,

face flushed with hatred for the man, who may well be the skin stripper in her mind."

Two hours later the man opened the door, they could see Taqi Al-Wahid, shake his hand from the safety of the doorway. The man climbed into his car and drove away.

Markku emailed a contact who returned the requested information, minutes later.

"Fucking odd? That car is registered to Sapo Verde. This web is growing by the hour. Let's see that photo."

She held her mobile phone to face him.

"That's good,"

They continued their observation for another two nights but the format never varied. The man in the Porsche never returned, but a van took away a large long box early one morning. With the 'accident' at the rear door, everything had to go via the main door at the front, an added bonus for Markku and his assistant.

"Let's wrap this up; there is nothing we can extract from this."

"Where to."

"Paris, I think I should check on the owner of that Porsche. I was heavily involved in that company, the woman who owns it has a past, but it is not her style to be connected with the scum in there." He pointed at the window across the road.

"And me?"

"Let's discuss it horizontally, back at the hotel."

"I have never had it put that way before."

"See, I also have a game called sex by numbers."

"I get that one; I guess 69 is your favourite number."

"No 47."

"What is a 47?"

"Oh, you Aussie girls need to travel more." His lecherous smile amusing her thoughts.

By morning, she wished she had never asked about a 47.

As Markku paid the hotel she ambled by the small kiosk in reception. There were newspapers and magazines from all over the World. She picked an English magazine called' Hello'. She flicked the pages and froze.

Markku walked across to her. "What's up?" He could read her look.

"It's him, look." She whispered.

On page 8 there was an article on the growth of the Bomy brand and several pictures of the two proud owners, taken in their Paris home.

Coco Cicorre stood beside her live in lover, as they described him.

The famous Parisian Lawyer, Michel Palatt.

Chapter 46

Paris, France.

Jacque Martell arrived at Coco's house in a chauffeured black Audi 8.

He was greeted by a nervous Ingrid Boaden, nervous because she knew Coco would poke fun at them all evening, her sense of humour sometimes a little too screwball. She loved her like a sister and had warned Jacque "She could be a bit off the wall at times."

Jacque was casually dressed, no business attire in his company, the emphasis on performance, not appearance detail.

Coco met them at the front door, and launched into her routine of making people feel comfortable and relaxed.

"Champagne Jacque?"

"Yes, is it a good brand, you know I am in the business." He joked

Coco reacted to his challenge; she turned the bottle and read the label. "It says made in Romania."

"Ah" he bantered back, "You can't beat a good gypsy's kiss Champagne."

Coco explained that Michel was running late, she had no reason why and the call from his mobile was brief, almost curt, and decidedly unemotional.

She was losing patience with him.

They waited an hour and an apologetic Michel

rushed through the door, condemning the French traffic system around Paris. "The Périphérique was a bloody nightmare tonight" he moaned. He shook hands with Jacque and saying "He wanted to freshen up, and would be down in 10 minutes.

Ingrid noticed, he did not kiss Coco hello.

The conversation was humorous and light, Coco warmed to the man and even Michel seemed more relaxed.

Coco went into detail about her Foundation plans, explaining she had yet to finalize the projects focus of support.

"What did Simon want from life?" Jacque asked.

Coco rambled a little, slightly embarrassed to extol his character too strongly in front of Michel.

"He cared about people, really cared, he never treated anybody as inferior, or asked anyone do anything he would n't do himself. He had respect I guess, He enjoyed life. That sums him up."

"So his Foundation should be a legacy for those who need help, maybe orphan kids, kids with terminal illness, that type of work." Jacques words echoed in her mind.

"I think Simon would have wanted to help those who have not lived a long life, kids with terminal cancer and the like, would be a perfect reflection of his attitude. He was always big on attitude. I think you have a brilliant idea Jacque. Thank you." She was on the verge of tears.

"Ingrid tells me you have funds donated already."

"Yes, two huge amounts and I have promised to match every donation from Sapo Verde. At present we stand at 4 million Euros."

"Make that 5 million." he smiled and passed a cheque across the table.

"Then it's 6million already! How fantastic", she yelled. "More champagne everyone."

At the end of the meal Jacque went to his car and returned with a special edition cognac. Martell XX, vintage. "You don't actually drink it, you put it somewhere prominent and boast about it a dinner parties." He laughed at his own joke.

"Not in this house." Said a happy Coco. Now you two, no snogging on the porch, so as the neighbours can see."

"Coco. Stop it." Ingrid grabbed his arm and hoisted him towards the door, both laughing at her matronly dictate.

Ingrid retuned and went straight to bed, aware the tension between the 2 was heavy. Now alone with Michel she tried to bring him out of his mood.

"I'm fine Coco, just tired, you know, it's so full on and I have n't had a break for a few months, maybe I will take a week out and go skiing."

He knew she would never go to the snow resorts, having lost her husband to a skiing accident in Andorra, nearly 30 years ago...

"That sounds a really good idea, but make sure you come back in one piece.

He cracked a joke for the first time in weeks. "Coming back in more than one piece sounds pretty awful, here's Michel's leg and oh, here comes the rest of him."

"You go up. I will try and tidy the kitchen a little."

She smiled, not a happy smile, one of worry and concern. Something was n't right.

Ten minutes later her mobile rang. She looked at her watch, wondering who would be calling at such a late hour.

"Hello."

"Coco its Rani." He sounded excited. "Sorry it's late for you but I just received the breakdown of the animal testing you suggested. The data is really powerful news. Of the 1000 animals, 765 rated over 81% before we started the tests. The others went from anywhere from 52% upwards. Under that and they are not really suitable for tests"

"So how did they all rate so highly after the tests?"

"ELG", it has to be ELG! Remember I mentioned the fermentation, it cleansed everything, it has the power to attack most, if not all, of the bacteria which remained. The core ELG has helped the animals rid their systems of bacteria and bone decease, everything. The scientists believe if we can get the fermentation steam controllable, for a longer period, it would be even more powerful. The long shot is it would almost certainly help humans, cancer, bone marrow issues and the leukaemia of this world."

"My God" she gasped. "How long."

"We are testing 5 dogs; who local vets were about to put down. We should see a reaction in weeks. Weeks. Is n't this fantastic?"

"More than that Rani. It could bring massive changes to millions of sick people's lives. I would like to support you through my Foundation in any way I can?"

"Let's talk; maybe I will come to Paris in a couple of weeks."

"That would be great; you are welcome to stay with us."

They said their farewells. Coco was too wide awake and excited. She walked to her private draw, unrolled a small plastic bag and rolled herself a joint. She picked a bottle of Spanish red from the rack and walked through to the terrace, cocooning herself in one of the big comfortable chairs, a blanket to keep out the chill air.

She held private conversations with Simon, as she floated back to 1973.

Chapter 47

Downing Street, London, England.

"PM." Timothy Jade poked his jaunty face around the half open door to the Cabinet Room. "Last two have arrived at the Gates Sir."

"OK, show them straight in and Tim, order some lunch for us all, it could be a long afternoon"

The Police Commissioner, Robert Dennis, and the Head of Special Branch, Charlie Holmes, 'Sherlock' to those in the Job, walked in stern faced and took their seats, alongside the full COBRA Group members.

"Prime Minister, I have just come off the phone with Captain Van Beleit of the Amsterdam Police. I regret to inform you, there has been another skin crucifixion, a second young girl was found in apartment after one of the neighbours' dogs would not stop barking at the door. Same MO."

The shock apparent on everyone's face.

"Any leads?" The PM grasping at straws.

"None really Prime Minister, we cannot see a link at the moment, other than we have unsubstantiated intelligence that Taqi Al-Wahid may be in Amsterdam. Charlie's boys are working flat out and I have sent one of them to work with our Dutch colleagues. It is a lengthy process running through video footage at airports and docks. The open borders offer us little help in these types of situations."

William Etherington had made a personal plea for the Press to combat their enthusiasm of the gory detail, only the Sun were reluctant, claiming newspapers, a mere 21 miles from Dover, across the English Channel, were relaying the graphic detail to their public. "Commissioner, what more can we do, is it a question of manpower, or are we having to sit on our thumbs until someone slips up?"

Slightly irritated, by the thumb referral, his reply was blunt. "We need more manpower; this is back to basic Police work, hours and hours of checks, however simple they maybe. It takes time. I am not sure the Dutch work the same way as us, and given the crime is on their patch, they not be too agreeable if I send in an army of helpers."

The door to the room knocked." Pardon the intrusion Sir; I have Scotland Yard needing to talk urgently with Mr Holmes."

The PM nodded approval to the Special Branch chief.

Charlie Holmes walked back into the room after a brief exchange with his department's Assistant Chief Superintendent. His features not in the Mona Lisa mould, creased and hard boned. Not a man to argue with.

"We have a lead." He spoke in a slow, direct manner, familiar Police self-control.

"French Police have received an anonymous tip off; they are currently surrounding a house in Paris, and will update us when they can."

"Good news." Beamed the stressed Prime Minister.

"Early days Sir." A calm, experienced response, from the Special Branch veteran.

The two Police Officers left the meeting after an hour,

frustrated at the pointless charade of ideas; TV programmes making the process of investigation appear simple, "Usually by a glamorous female with a models figure and too much breast showing." He added, grunting towards Charlie Holmes. "How to catch the perpetrator of this heinous crime can only be from intelligence and forensics, and loads of bloody leg work."

As they passed Big Ben their Police driver took a call. "Mr Holmes, it's for you Sir." He handed the phone to the back seats.

"Holmes."

"OK, damn."

There was a pause as he listened to the rest of the relay. "Don't worry Bernart; we get the same crank calls here. You need to worry more about coming to Twickenham this weekend; our boys are on fire this season."

He waited again, and signed off in friendly Police jargon

"Will they bollocks!"

"Crank call Sir, man fingered is a top Paris Lawyer, Michel Palatt, he runs Sapo Verde, the huge international empire. Pucker, upright citizen."

"Hmnn, so was Lord Lucan."

"Shall I tell the PM?"

"No. not yet, let them dream up some ideas for us we are bound not

to have thought of. Just to cover all angles, and the Politics, whizz over to Paris and chat with the boys there, it may be pointless, but I've got a hunch."

He tapped his drivers shoulder," Light her up Aryton,

we are busy men." The piercing tunes exploded into life, hidden 'blues' in the headlamps of the unmarked Jaguar frightening the traffic in front of them. To add presence, the driver, using one hand, clamped a larger blue light on the roof. The acceleration was instant as they carved open their own lane.

"Look miserable Charlie, no one likes to see a happy copper!"

As they approached Scotland Yard the Commissioners' mobile bleeped. He looked at the caller ID.

"He we go, its bloody Etherington, bet he says we should call fucking Starsky and Hutch!"

Chapter 48

Paris, France.

Markku and Karin had walked past the house four times in the last two hours. It was still only 6.45am and the lights had only just come on downstairs in the hall-way.

Markku stopped still, gripping Karin's hand tightly. "Company."

She turned her head slowly to the right as four navy blue trucks entered the street.

"Wait." He whispered.

She felt the shiver run through her body and reached for her firearm, concealed inside the pocket of the Burberry raincoat she had purchased in Amsterdam.

The convoy of trucks and a black Citroen raced alongside them and flooded the entrance of the house. Armed Police swarmed from the trucks in unison and took up their pre-planned positions. More marked Police cars had sealed the road and three men in blue military style uniforms were running towards them. They made little noise but urged them to run towards them.

The obeyed and once they cleared the safety of the cars they stopped. "We should wait and watch, that is what normal people would do, wait until they tell us to go. Be natural." She snuggled against him in fake fear.

"Not that natural." He grinned as she let her hand roam inside his jacket.

They watched the Police vehicles as they drove away, the man from the Porsche sandwiched between 2 broad shouldered Para Military types.

"Now how did they get onto him before us?" Markku was holding a fierce debate in his head. Karin skipped along in front of him, teasing the man.

"Guess we got the day off then?"

Markku was battling his demons, demons of distrust.

Chapter 49

Paris, France.

Inspector Bernart Gris had worked out of the Paris 'Hilton' Police HQ for 23 years. The building was old fashioned and reminded him of hospitals when he was 5 or 6. Across the street he had watched the new Headquarters building rise from deep foundations over the last 4 years. Too late for him, he would retire, before they all walked across the street, at end of the year.

Gris and a team of Para Military officers had surrounded the large house from early morning. The man they were seeking was pinned down as he left, just before 8.30am.

"Had to be a fucking top Lawyer, some bastard set us up." He flicked at the peeling wall paper, edged around the rear of the school sized radiator he was perched on. "JP! Any news on that trace."

JP rushed into the room. Fontainebleau Sir, It's a Mental Hospital Sir.

"Oh, Bollocks. A genuine nutter then. Thanks."

He threw the newly created card file in the bin. "I suppose I will get dragged into the torture chamber and demoted, once the friggin Lawyer gets hold of Top Dog.

Their slang, unusual, as with every institutional system.

Charlie Holmes arrived at the Paris 'Hilton' HQ just before 7.00pm.

Bernart Gris waited for his English colleague with anticipation. Charlie liked a glass or two of wine, and he expected they would discuss the case and then hit La Coupol for the evening. They had worked together many times on serious cross border crimes, the joint success was the result of their relationship and trust.

"Hi Bernart, I didn't expect to see you when I searched for me socks in the dark this morning."

"Ah you English have no control over your women, mine has everything laid out for me each morning. "The banter of friendship, and camaraderie.

They both had the same disgust about the skin crucifixions, the French papers had published graphic shots of the girl in Amsterdam causing anger on the streets, and suspicion directed towards the big Muslim community. Parts of the City were almost deserted as the Police feared a backlash from within the chased communities.

They drove to La Coupol and settled in a booth, watching people attempt impossible feats, with huge tiered platters of seafood.

"What do think of this shit then Bernart?"

"I am divided; the call today wasted hours of our time, turns out it came from some friggin nutjob in a mental home."

"Jesus, don't they limit access to outside calls in these places anymore?"
No, I think you get free Blackberry when you sign up! They laughed at the cruel humour. Police work always needs an outlet, alcohol, sex, or black comedy lines. They all understood the rules.

"Has anyone interviewed the person who made the call?"

"No, the call was made from Fontainebleau; once we had the address we abandoned it as a hoax."

"Mind if I try in the morning?"

"Be my guest, not much else to go on. Need a shotgun rider?"

"Good idea, I would probably get hopelessly lost, trying to find the place anyway."

Charlie staggered into the Mercury Hotel just after 2.00am.

Five hours later, the bedside alarm jerked him into a new day. He felt dry, and he felt old.

Bernart picked him up in a large Citroen and they headed toward Fontainebleau, ignoring the speed limits. Twenty minutes later Bernart pulled into a service area and suggested breakfast. Charlie was relieved and welcomed the strong coffee, ignoring the croissants and pastries.

The gravel driveway at the Hospital is long, with manicured gardens to both sides. The Chateau is impressive and grand; Charlie blew a whistle of admiration. "Must cost a bundle to stay here."

"It's not a hotel Charlie." The French copper laughed. "Once you get in, that's usually that. Life stops here."

"Seen a lot worse."

They parked the car and entered the building, which was modern inside, conflicting with the ornate posture of the exterior. It was spotlessly clean.

They waited for the senior Doctor to finish his phone

call.

He replaced the handset and walked to the small waiting area to see why he had 2 senior Police visitors.

"Good morning." He opened his hands and exchanged pleasantries. I am Doctor Clement.

Bernart introduced his colleague, boldly adding, "From Scotland Yard." The two seasoned officers picked up the raised eyebrow, usually a sign of surprise at the prestigious name.

He invited them into his office and ordered coffees.

Bernart explained they had traced a malicious call from the hospital to Paris Police HQ the previous day, and whilst he fully understood the difficulty with the type of patient they cared for, it still needed to be followed up.

The Doctor immediately held his hand up. "I know I know. We have a patient who has been here 11 years; she is a tragic case and barely speaks to anyone. Her mind is locked in a period of time we cannot, up until now that is, deflect her from. She has stood against a wall singing songs by the English man George Michael, since the day she arrived.

She made a determined attempt at suicide when her 6-month old daughter disappeared in 1987. She failed and was sectioned here.

In these tragic cases, there is often a trigger, which releases a part of the brain, which has been confining activity to a limited memory or vocabulary. We try hard to find the release of course, but it is not easy, medication is usually the only option, to give the patient some reasonable quality of life."

Charlie placed his empty cup on the desk. "You said, until now."

"Yes, she was watching the TV news 2 nights ago and they were running a piece on the girls who are being killed, the skin crucifixions, I believe they are called?"

"Correct." Bernart nodded.

"All of a sudden she exploded in rage. Of course, this is a daily occurrence in places such as ours. She ran to her room and barricaded herself in, screaming she wanted to talk to her husband."

"And she had never acted this way previously?" Charlie impatiently fiddled with his watch strap.

"Never. As I said she has hardly done anything, other than sing to the wall for 11 years."

"So what did you do?"

"I was n't here. This happened late evening but we have a drill, or procedure, in particular when we feel someone could self-harm themselves. The nurses dealt with it and upped her dose to calm her, we had to inject her on the floor, which is unsavoury and can set other patients off. "

"I dunno how you do it Doctor" said Charlie. "How many actually return to a normal life?"

"Sadly a very small number. It is tragic but we all care for these people, and do what we can."

Bernart joined the conversation "Presumably she managed to call our office, how could that happen?

"I am not sure. I was discussing the same question with her husband when you arrived."

"Thank you doctor; it seems straight forward. For the

record what is the woman's name?"

"Mrs Heidi Palatt. Her husband is a famous Lawyer in Paris. Michel Palatt."

Inspector Bernart Gris shivered. He looked at Charlie. His eyes registering sudden renewed interest in Mr Palatt.

"May we talk with Mrs Palatt?"

"You would need to come back in the morning gentlemen, we have her heavily sedated, you will not get any decipherable reasoning from her today.

The two Policemen walked back to their Citroen in silence. As Bernart started the engine he turned to Charlie, "What do you think?"

"Do you understand the expression 'I smell a rat'?"

"Yeah, I do, a rich, fat rat, in this instance."

"I had better phone home."

"Like ET eh?"

"Yes, just like ET."

Chapter 50

Paris, France.

Coco felt for Michel, his wife had caused him so much distress over the last 11 years; here she was planning an afternoon's sex with a notorious womanizer whilst he suffered the ignominy of answering questions about killing girls in Holland.

As she told the Inspector "He was here, we had dinner with Jacque Martell and Ingrid Boaden. She is upstairs and I am confident Jacque will collaborate the story with a quick call."

Michel was released after less than an hour at the Police HQ and returned home. She comforted him and reiterated, "Maybe you should go on the skiing trip, you have had more than your share of crap this week."

The truth is she wanted him out of the way as she battled with her thoughts; they bounced between her needs and the care she should show to Michel. Energised sex with Bjorn kept winning the ping pong match.

Michel took his opportunity and spent 10 minutes on the phone. He booked a week in Zermatt, Switzerland, leaving later that day.

Coco booked a car to take her to the meeting with Bjorn and they discussed several interesting ideas for the Hotel Party night in New York. His contacts in the music business ensured they would have A-rated guests galore on the night.

"Probably a ratio of 3 to 1 in favour of women." she questioned.

They finished lunch in the beautiful surroundings of the George V restaurant.

"What time is Star arriving?"

"About 5, she is coming with her Mother to sign the contracts with Michel's old Lawyers firm, and then we all fly off to London for a couple of days recording."

She looked at her watch.

"Blimey, is that new?"

"Yes, Rani gave it to me as a present when I saw him in Japan. I had admired his one when we were in Cannes and he remembered. Sweet of him."

The huge black faced U-Boat watch dominated her wrist.

"I better get one so as I keep up with the trendy ones." he said.

She stared at him. "I am nervous about this."

"So am I. Want another drink?"

"I can't do it Bjorn. I just can't. I want to, I really want to. We have been friends for so long, and it is my loss." She touched his thigh, feeling the energy crackle between them.

His face distorted a little and he blew out his cheeks, "Let's go for a walk I need some air?"

He continued talking as they left the room. "I have been thinking of this afternoon all night, hell, I am so horny. That will teach me." He rolled his eyes upwards towards the ornate ceiling and slipped a hand over hers.

"Let's keep the powder dry and take a rain check."

She thought she understood the message and agreed. She pecked his cheek as cameras flashed on the pavement outside.

"Oh! Look he yelled it's my Star. She's early"

The hordes of press and freelance photographers were barging people out of the way, forming a scrum for a lucrative picture of Bjorn's new teen sensation.

Star was bundled through the doors by the Hotel security and a catcall to Bjorn drifted across the melee.

"What you going to do about the writ from Starbucks?"

"What fucking writ?" Bjorn faked a hopelessly poor surprised expression, having been advised of the writ the previous day. He smiled as his plan started to evolve. Over lunch, Coco had agreed the second and slightly provocative phase of the plan.

Star fell against Bjorn and he grabbed her towards protective arms. "You look fantastic babe."

Star smouldered and pressed her young frame against his body; she looked up and said "Hi Babe to Coco."

They were swept further into the hotel foyer as the crush of press had attracted young onlookers; all anxious to get a view of the girl they called Star Buck.

Star turned," Where is she, where's my Mum."

"I'm here darling." Coco and Bjorn turned together, and came face to face with a dead girl.
Bjorn was shocked and stared in disbelief.

"Melanie." Coco collapsed against a pillar, face white and eyes fixed.

The pandemonium of shock sent a flurry of questions bouncing into the air, Bjorn was visibly shaking and Coco moved towards Melanie Preston in an aggressive manner, eyes narrowing and body rigid.

The Hotel security had no warning the sudden out-pouring of antagonism, the meeting of old enemies would spark. They were trying to clear the lobby of fans and press, the stand-off in the corner was likely to erupt any second. Press photographers held cameras high trying to catch a shot of the young female Star, who appeared to have triggered the unseemly pushing match.

Aaron Milan hid in the coffee lounge watching the explosion he knew may come one day. He could not intervene until the press mob had been evicted.

As the journalists and their photographers were finally manhandled through the famous doors, they still had sporadic attempts by fans to gain entrance.

Bjorn had managed to pull Star to safety and thinking as quickly as ever approached the head of security, who was busy calling for Police help.

"Dion, let the fans in, there are only 15 or so, we can take them to a room and let them talk with Star, if will quell the tension out there and help with this little situation" He jerked a finger towards the bitter exchanges taking place between Coco and Melanie.

"OK, Bjorn, whatever you say, this is not what we want at our hotel."

"Yeah, not much," Bjorn thought he turned towards the security man. "It will be all over the press and TV by tonight, we would n't want anything like that would we?"

His craggy smile producing a grin from Dion Poise.

The young fans were invited in and although their number suddenly swelled to nearly 30 it was a sensible solution. Bjorn stayed with Star to ensure they were not at risk. The security found them a large meeting room and the excited teenagers awaited their new hero, with a respectful patience.

Bjorn seated the fans and with security in place he was happy Star would be able to dominate the fans. He ran back to the foyer. The situation had calmed and he could see Coco and Melanie walking down a corridor with a man he did not know. He called out "Hey, ladies, is everything OK?"

The man turned and walked back to Bjorn. "We are going to my suite, the girls and I have a great deal to discuss." Coco mouthed an "It's OK" towards Bjorn. "What suite are you in?"

"The Royal, come up when you have dealt with the fans, nice work Mr Free."

Bjorn scampered back to the room, finding Anita and Sian had arrived and the whole situation changed.

Star was chatting to fans and signing autographs, they turned as Bjorn walked in and he took command, posing with young girls, hands roaming in his normal suggestive way and kisses planted, just too close to teenage lips, for any protective parent. He was loving the moment, but wanted to know about Melanie and the strange man.

In the Royal Suite, Aaron Milan had subdued the anger between the women.

"This is a long, long story, which will be hard for Coco to understand Melanie."

She nodded. "I know, go ahead, it is cleared." She sat impassive on the couch next to her old friend.

His background to the sudden and alarming meeting went back beyond 1973. "Melanie was from a very wealthy German family, she lived in Munich as a child and sent to England for schooling, her family life was minimal and she had little contact with her parents. She was a product of the true English gentry system, schooled at Roedean in Sussex and groomed by one of the best finishing Schools in Switzerland. Her real name is Gisela Baumann. Her brother was one of the leading members of Baader-Meinhof, the German terror organization.

Their actions were seen by many as terrorism, by others, more intellectual people they were viewed as fore-runners to an organization called Gadosh Mitsvah, which exists today.

Badder-Meinhof tried to deflect the perception of their aims and formed a splinter group called Schwarze Zelle, Black Cell in English. This parallel group took on the mantle of fear within Germany but the bulk of their members were drifters, or drug addicts simply bent on disruption and chaos tactics. Baader Meinhof silenced their own sister organization, but with the agreement of the German government, gave the credit to Israel. Israel had few friends so the negatives were minimal.

Baader Meinhof evolved into Gadosh Mitsvah, as we know it today, it is a Jewish sounding name but it is not a Jewish only organization, maybe organization is also a misleading term?

Gadosh Mitsvah followed the real long term objective set out all those years ago but sadly misinterpreted at the time, they were not maniac hard line terrorists and neither are today's people.

Governments around the World have let their own people down repeatedly, often ill prepared to take action because they seek personal gain from their own democratic selection, others who came to power via the family, or dictator bullyboy method, run their Countries on fear and retain lavish lifestyles at the expense of the masses.

General Toyo from Japan, witnessed the Hiroshima bombs effects the day after the Americans dropped it. He helped create the group that exists today, whose aim is to eradicate the dictators of fear, eradicate the chances of terrorist groups ever reaching the power to start a World War, and to prevent a day like Hiroshima suffered, from ever happening again.

Gisela, Melanie as you know her, joined us early in 1970. She was what we call a decoy, her mission to infiltrate the growing mafia in Spain. Carglinas was heavily linked to General Franco, his team often carried out sadistic killings in return for animosity and free passage in all of the high income fields of Tourism. She was undercover until 1995 when, with others she plotted the downfall of Sapo Verde and the Carglinas woman. This commitment is hard to understand for you I am sure Coco. "She nodded having listened intently.

He looked at Melanie, "It is the only way forward Gisela."

Melanie asked him to continue.

"We have a layer system, we have an Executive of 4 people, I am the link between field agents and the executive, and we act on our own although major decisions are usually referred. Each field agent has his or her own people, but nobody used their own name. Everyone has to pass a wealth inspection, we do not pay anyone and we do not allow money to be a disruption to an agent's work, or decisions."

"Now to sum up, it is very difficult for you to understand what I am about to say, very difficult." Coco looked overwhelmed.

"Go on" she said softly, head down.

"We knew the situation you were in with Carglinas, Gisela and I had many discussions on a bail out, but the operation was vital to the next few years. We knew Simon would receive a heavy sentence; we would have then set about lobbying to get him released, once we had the proof of the corrupt regime. Sadly, we had no idea you and he would reach such an unorthodox agreement, the decision for you to kill him, and in turn presumably kill yourself, left us all in shock, Melanie more than anyone."

Coco glanced across at Melanie.

Aaron continued. "When you were released from Cadiz we had two other people from Gadosh Mitsvah working for Sapo Verde, they were there for your protection and our chance to make amends, which we did in terms of financial and the Company which was rightly yours and Simons. Maria, the head girl for Los Ricos, is also one of our people. She protected you in the prison as many times there was call to terminate you.

"Our aim at the present time is far removed from your current situation but you are high on our radar. We want you to consider joining us in our goal to help the World become a better, fairer place, and safer. This means you have a decision to make, not easy. We will talk to you more in the next few weeks but the World is under serious threat at the moment and Governments are unable to thwart the modern terrorist."

There was silence in the room. "Here is my number," he passed her a card with several numbers listed. "There is a huge risk for us talking to you today; Melanie was the person who instigated this challenge. Melanie is no longer a field agent; she is a member of the Executive of Gadosh Mitsvah.

Please call me; we need forward thinking people on our Executives.

"I am a little drained by the day's events; my partner was arrested this morning and then released; now it appears they are searching for him again. Someone I thought I knew well. Like I thought I knew Melanie well back in the seventies, like I don't know her at all now, because her name is Gisela and she is someone different to the person I have hated for nearly 30 years. I must go; I will not discuss this with anyone and will be in contact. I am in shock." Coco's face flushed with anger.

He walked her to the door meeting Bjorn waiting patiently outside.

"You OK babe?"

"I have no fucking idea if I am OK, upside down, inside out. Are you guys still going to London tonight?"

"No we are staying here, put the session back couple of days."

"Ring me tonight Bjorn, I need a friend."

He kissed her on the cheek. "Sure babe. Love ya."

She smiled. "Me to."

Chapter 51

Fontainebleau, France.

The two Police Officers arrived at the Hospital at 10.00am. The van which had followed them down with 4 additional officers was parked half a mile away, just as a precaution.

They were greeted by the same doctor who took them through the residents lounge area. Several patients were walking about, focused in their own World, some talking to themselves, others having banal conversations with their imagined friends. A few glanced at the two policemen but generally no one paid attention. Two men were arguing at a corner table, raised voices, neither of them listening to the others opinion. Had it been a Pub someone would have stopped them long ago, but here it was par. Suddenly the taller of the two men stepped up his vocals and grabbed a chair lifting it above his head. He hurled the plastic chair towards the second man who caught the full force as it smashed into his shoulder. He verbally retaliated but did not attack the aggressor. The tension dissipated and the room calmed. In the temperament of the large room, no one seemed to notice the flare up and continued reading or watching a silent TV.

The Police officers ignored the incident, as did the smiling staff who were preparing the mornings medication; expectant faces circled the hatch in the wall, anxious for their first fix of the day.

Heidi Palatt was dressed in a thin floral print dress. Her hair carried her signature little bows, but several strands of hair fell across her face, promoting a vacant look.

She stood up as they entered the room. "Good afternoon gentleman." Her miscalculated time ignored by the 2 men in suits.

"Hello Mrs Palatt" Bernart introduced himself and using the template introduced the man next to him as being from 'Scotland Yard.

"Oh gosh, "she muttered, "Scotland Yard."

Charlie smiled. "She looks pretty 'with it' to me." he thought.

"I assume you have come about my phone call and the murders involving those poor girls. I can tell you everything you need to know. I can tell you my husband did these terrible crimes and I can tell you of others, from years back. The recent events I have no knowledge, sadly."

Bernart looked at the Doctor. He nodded for her to continue.

"I married Michel because I was expecting a child, he was never happy with the marriage, but my parents were strict Jehovah Witnesses, having a child outside of Wedlock is one of the most hennas crimes, according to their strict beliefs. We married and I had a girl. Rose we called her. It was a pretty name don't you think?

The three men smiled approval.

He, Michel, had told me of his interest in 'skinning' as he called it, but if I challenged him he would become violent and threaten to skin me. He started once,"

She lifted her dress and the right thigh had what looked like

burn scar.

"He did this, just to frighten me. He would bring girls home, young girls, always cheaply dressed, short skirts, silly high heels they could n't walk in. They all looked like ladies of the night to me."

The Policemen remained silent, allowing her to gather her thoughts.

She continued. "We never made love around the times when he brought girls home. Never. I knew what was coming once he stopped the sex, he was quite demanding normally. If 10 days went by I knew he would bring a girl home." She started to cry.

"Maybe we should leave this." The doctor coldly interrupted by Bernart.

"Let her speak. Heidi, what happened with the girls he took home?"

She sniffled and carried on. "He would have sex with them, always made me watch. Some were so young. Then he would take them to the cellar, it had to be below ground level for some reason. In the cellar I would hear their screams as he peeled their skin off. He would leave them to die, hanging from the beam. Sometimes it took 3 days, others sooner.

"What did you do with the bodies?"

"We sealed them in the cellar, after he skinned Rose in a temper."

The Doctor ran from the room, face pale and sickly, the veterans of crime hardly registered their disgust, anxious to continue the detail, in fear she would slip back into the world she had shared with George Michael, for 11 years.

She was sobbing now but they offered no comfort, she had to expel the story for them. "After Rose died, we sealed the cellar and sold the house. I decided to kill myself but God saved me I guess. I have been here 11 years the doctor said before you came. Why in all that time did nobody sing back to me?"

Charlie as worried they would lose her. "Where was the house, where the girls and Rose were buried?"

"Paris of course."

"Of course" he echoed. "Do you remember the address?"

"Yes. 48, Rue Mendel. Near the Arc. It was a wonderful house."

"Thank you Heidi."

"Can I go home now?"

"You had better see the Doctor about that."

They walked back to the doctor's office. He was sitting on the chair behind his immaculate desk. He had dark rings under his eyes and had been crying. "You OK doc?" asked Charlie.

"What now? I cannot believe Michel Palatt would do such things."

Bernart called his Paris office and relayed the story just told by Heidi Palatt. "Pick him up immediately; any females in that house are in grave danger."

They raced back to the house in Paris, touching 150 mph at times, claxon changing tune, every few hundred yards.

Ten miles from Paris a call to Bernart informed them that Michel Palatt had left for Zermatt for a week's skiing.

"Is his partner with you?"

"Yes."

"Good, I need to talk with her."

"Inspector, she has had her doctor here for an hour or so, her day has got steadily worse."

"We will be 20 minutes, tops."

They arrived at Coco's house to find a full scale operation in place. Charlie walked ahead and saw Coco sitting in a chair, faced burnt with pain. Ingrid Boaden was trying to comfort her.

Bernart took over. "I am sorry Miss Cicorre, but I need to ask you a few really personal questions and I know this has all come as a shock."

She nodded.

"Have you and Michel had a normal sex life in recent days, say 10 or 12 days."

"No sex." She cried softly.

"Can't this wait Inspector?" Ingrid begged.

"Sorry ma'am but there is a huge risk Michel may kill again tonight."

Charlie leaned towards Ingrid, "Can we chat in the kitchen?"

In the tidy kitchen he told Ingrid of the story told them by Michel's wife. The outline of the story made her feel sick. "Oh God, she was in such danger, all this time. We can't stay here tonight; do you mind if I call a friend."

She called Jacque and he hurried to Coco's house.

The two women left with him an hour later.

Bernart Gris slumped in his office chair. "He didn't take that flight Charlie, we checked and he was a no show."

"Bollocks" said the man from the Yard, "Any guess where he maybe."

"Could be anywhere, the Zermatt booking could have been a diversion"

"Can we check his phone calls?"

"Being done now, I reckon he is on the run, but where to?"

20 minutes later they received confirmation of no additional calls and no record in his name of any flights leaving France.

"My guess is he is travelling by car. Can we circulate details?"

"Yeah, will do Charlie, I may use the press on this one, the public are behind us, for a fucking change."

Chapter 52

Paris, France.

Markku and Karin were lying on a bed in a large chain hotel, close to the Eiffel Tower. She had suggested they take the tourist trip to the iconic landmark, but he had other things on his mind.

It was nearing lunch and they had spent the morning making love, the chambermaid had been turned away twice, amid giggles from the other maids, mostly of Senegal decent.

"Aside from that it is raining." he argued.

They had the TV set to Sky News and followed each update on the skin crucifixion story, the regularity, prolonging their sexual activity, as they stopped to listen.

The good looking presenter was talking from outside Coco Cicorre's palatial house, and the latest news quote from the Police was they were still looking for Michel Palatt and that all flights leaving France were being checked. The public were asked not to approach him as he is considered dangerous, the usual blurb.

Markku sat upright, lifting naked Karin away. "I think he's heading back to Amsterdam again."

"Is that a calculated guess?" She was already dressing.

"No, he is on the run; TV has the detail so the cops are trying to flush him out. He can't stay in Paris; he is too well known. He will be in his Porsche heading to Amsterdam, hoping to satisfy the sexual craving of killing and skinning young girls. You get back to Amsterdam as fast as you can, just steal a car, nothing too flash as it will have tracker and the roads will be watched tonight, Drive like mad. If he is there let me know. I have an errand to run this end, stay in touch." They kissed goodbye, still glowing from the lazy morning's passion.

Karin walked outside and turning down a narrow cobbled side street she saw a Mercedes SLK sports car." Just right for me, nice girlie car." She joked with herself and looked around, and then checked inside. "Oh cool, bonus points today Karin, its steering is on the right." The car was on British plates and she joined the dodgems circuit around the Arc de Triomphe before settling into a fast drive to Amsterdam.

Markku called Aaron and he confirmed a meeting the following morning in Paris.

Karin touched 140 mph in the car, but rain started to fall as she crossed in to Holland and the traffic slowed. She reached the Pink house and circled the block, from both directions, three times. It all seemed quiet, that usually converted to danger and she was acutely aware of the need to follow the 'rule of life' book. Hell, she knew the author personally, very personally.

She parked the car 200 yards away, and walked in the shadow to the rear of the Pink house. She studied every floor window for several minutes each, she checked for lighting flickering in rooms, as best she could, but it was still a dangerous gamble. She edged closer to the rear doors, her gun in her left hand and the spare mobile bomb in her rear pocket. She opened the door without disturbing sound, opened her phone close to the first step and scanned the coffee particles they had scattered on the last two steps, before their last departure. The pale light from her phone screen formed a square on the step and she noticed a foot print in the coffee granules, it was facing into the stair, meaning someone had been in there since she and Paul had. She closed the phone and took one step every 3 minutes, listening for sounds and wary of being followed in from the shadows. The slowness of her cautious system meant it took her an hour to climb the stairway to the top floor.

She reached the room they had occupied and crawled to the window. It was late and if the regular evening's entertainment had been set up, she would be in time. She set up the camera to record the events across the road and for Paul to be able to see the same pictures via the new web cam system he had received from Japan.

She lifted her head above the window ledge and gasped, every window opposite had a man with eyes trained on her window. She had been spotted. She looked down; armed men were already streaming from the front door towards the rear of the Pink house trapping her in the building. She dialled Paul.

"I am compromised, they have me trapped on the top floor and my only chance is a gun fight, but the odds are stacked, there must be 10 or 12 of them.

"Is the Porsche there?"

"Yes, bang outside."

"Is the webcam in place?"

"Yes,"

"Turn it round to face the room and stay on the phone, I can be your second eyes."

She rushed to the window and turned the camera to face inside the room. "I have you". He confirmed. "They have one attack route; how much ammunition do you have?"

"3 clips and the mobile."

"Save the mobile until you have numbers"

"OK."

There was silence. She whispered, "They are close." She moved to the door and checked the stairs. She could see 3 men climbing slowly, guns stiffly stretched out in front of them, all looked nervous.

"Stay calm." She read the manual in her head.

She looked again, they had made slow progress. Her phone was clipped to her ear and Paul was gently calming her. "Breathe slowly."

The third look was a pattern number for action. She rolled to the floor and let go a burst of three shots. The noise in the empty building echoed and the in the flash of light she saw 4 more men on the stairway, 10 feet behind the three. None of the first three let off a shot and their screams meant she had hit at least 2.

She was calm and talking quietly to Paul. "Move back in case they rush you."

She stepped back into the camera room. There was little sound coming from the hallway. She crept back to the door after a few minutes and looked out. Nothing.

She spoke to Paul. "What do you reckon?"

"Sit tight, these clowns are amateurs, stay cool and you can get out."

They waited on respective phones. The minutes ticked by.

Outside the door a sudden movement and loud noise. "They are charging" she cried to Paul.

He watched in horror on the web cam as he witnessed 5 men assault the doorway forcing their way in. Karin fired, hit the first three but was hammered to the floor by a burly man and pinned in a wrestlers hold. Paul watched on helplessly.

The last man to enter the room was Michel Palatt. He looked grey and strained, slurring his words appearing to be at the very edge of sanity. He looked down at the fallen girl, and told the men to, "get her up."

They grabbed her by the hair and lifted her to an upright position.

"Strip her."

Leering men tore the clothes from her and he could see Michel Palatt opening a small leather pouch. He saw the glint of a sharp instrument and the fear on her face. He was going to skin her. She was now naked and the other men circled her like hyena, staring at her fit body tone.

Michel Palatt had removed his trousers and underwear and stood in front of her, his manhood proudly displayed from beneath his shirt.

"Through the speaker system of the advanced technology webcam, he heard Michel say," A test trim before I fuck you, and then downstairs to the cellar."

He stepped forward and sliced a 3inch line beside her

left breast, he turned at the bottom dragging the cut across by an inch, as skilled as any surgeon.

"Karin scream nullified by the tennis ball forced into her mouth. Michel peeled the first rectangle of skin away and held it aloft like a trophy. He motioned to the men to force her backwards onto a table and stepped towards her, erect and holding his penis as the others forced her to accept him.

Markku had primed his computer and had his finger over the last digit of the mobile bomb, which was lying in her jean pocket, cast to the floor by the animal instinct of the group.

He screamed at the speaker on his split screen laptop, "Palatt! You are about to die."

Michel Palatt swung to the window expecting to see someone. All he heard was 'goodbye.' The room exploded, killing everyone, including Karin Moore.

Chapter 53

Paris, France.

Bernart and Charlie were sitting in the canteen, grabbing a late snack and coffee before they called it a night.

Bernart mobile rang. "Gris."

He listened facial muscle twitched and he grimaced. He folded his flip top Motorola back into his jacket pocket. "The Dutch boys have found his car; it was parked opposite a building which was bombed 2 hours ago."

Charlie groaned. "Someone has got to him before us?"

"You think so?"

"I know so my friend, this reeks of a man we have been chasing around the World for several months. He is like a superhero vigilante, if he finds a target he would blow up the whole building to make sure he succeeds. Innocents part of the ball game."

"Does he have a name?" Bernart looked bemused at this late revelation from the English cop.

"Name? He doesn't even have a face on our radar, we call him the Magician. Sounds like he's up to his old tricks again." His coarse laugh changed the atmosphere. "Fancy a beer Bern?"

"I thought you would never ask."

They climbed into his Citroen and headed towards the narrow streets near the Montmartre area seeking a small but friendly bar.

They had just settled against the bar when Charlie's mobile interrupted the Police language, always about the job.

"Yeah" Charlie sounded annoyed, his need for alcohol had increased over the last few years and the 'addiction' in his throat was like adrenalin to him.

He listened to the voice, face colouring by the second. "God almighty."

He covered the phone and called Bernart nearer, whispering a replay of the conversation. "The Yard has just received a video of Michel Palatt part skinning a girl and then as he was about to rape her, the tape cut. The last tiny frame was a flash, probably the explosion."
" Fucking hell Charlie, who are we dealing with here? Can they forward the video on line?"

Charlie asked the question. His rage exploded at the response. "Of course I won't fucking let anyone see it!"

He listened to the Yard man and turned toward Bernart. "Where shall they send it Bern?"

"Let's not waste time getting to my shop." He leaned over the counter, producing his Police ID to the landlord. "Have you got email here?"

He passed the address to the 2 Police Officers and the three of them went behind the bar, into his private accommodation, to wait for the video.

A few minutes passed and the landlord's laptop indicated a new message. They ushered the helpful man from his own lounge and watched the horror unfold. Neither man commented.

The final frame was as mentioned on the phone and

Charlie assumed the boys at the yard would be searching stills for clues. "First rule." He barked, "Never assume!" He called the Yard, and made sure they were following guidelines. The irritated person at the end of the line said "Of course, Sir."

Charlie ended the call. "Admin wally."

"We need to get to Amsterdam." He was staring at the hand written address of the bombing. "This address is in the same friggin street as the last contact we had for Taqi Al-Wahid. We have been staking the place for a few weeks, gotta a girl from Australian anti-terrorist department working with us, she's been deep for nearly 2 years chasing him, and the Magician. I would bet my pension that was her."

"Do you mean the girl has infiltrated Insha'Allah? "

"No, not quite. She had filters that did, the skinned body in Copenhagen, one of hers apparently. She has gotten close to the Magician, but we haven't had any contact since she got back from Australia a few weeks back." He was thinking, hand itching his stubble.

"I take that back about me pension by the way, bit too hasty there." He laughed; his 'coppers nose' had started to twitch.

Bernart deleted the email from the landlord's computer. As soon as they left the landlord raced upstairs to his 15-year-old son's bedroom. He was lying on the bed with a copy of Hustler magazine open in front of him. The landlord ignored the glamour shots of naked girls and rattled the keyboards of his son's laptop. His old Sony laptop, passed down 6 months ago still received his emails.

The young man had tucked the magazine under the covers and was uninterested in his Fathers email account.

"Bloody hell" the Landlord held a hand across his mouth. "Jesus Christ." Despite his son's protestations' he raced downstairs to his office and within minutes started a bidding war with the French press and TV channels.

Bernart had called for a Police helicopter to fly them to Amsterdam and as they sped through the late night traffic towards the heliport, they battered theories around the car.

Chapter 54

Fontainebleau, France.

Pieter Muller looked tired, he had just returned from a 48 hour round trip to Newcastle, Australia. The trip had been enjoyable apart from the travel.

He had used ELG-9 for the first time in solo and the effects impressed his technical brain. The area he wiped out extended 2 square miles beyond the planned 3 square miles, mostly bush but focused on Amy's Tavern and the housing estate nearby.

In his report to Aaron that evening in Paris, he raised concerns about the stability of the liquid, but enjoyed the mission.

Tonight's was easy for him, sadly none of the violence, which spiked his life, but it was all to do with the overall strategy, so he was compliant, if the fucking woman in the spare bedroom would stop singing he could turn down his own TV volume, currently used to drown the sound of her George Michael lyrics.

A week before his trip to Australia he had broken into the Mental hospital and with the Lebanese girl, Yaheem recently pulled from the Amsterdam house, as his partner, they had kidnapped Heidi Palatt. Using an actor quality prosthetic face, and her clothes, Yaheem had replaced her 'at the wall' for the few days before she was given the green light to start the operation to expose the rich Lawyer. Her clothing loose with tall knee length socks hid the skin tone difference. Doctor Clement had provided full sets of keys for the 'break in.' He was a one of the many wealthy supporters, of the organizations vast web of intelligent individuals.

Heidi had been held in a small house 5 kilometres outside Fontainebleau, a rural location barely touched by modern day services. She had continued to sing, albeit to an open plan audience, of farm animals, trees and fields.

Tonight, she would be drugged and placed in her bed, waking in the morning as if nothing had happened. Tomorrow, Doctor Clement would call Inspector Gris in Paris, informing him she had relapsed back into her trance like George Michael obsession.

Chapter 55

Amsterdam, Holland

The Pink building was in a dangerous condition, Bernart Gris and Charlie Holmes picked their way through the rubble looking up towards the missing top three floors. More rubble bounced to the ground and once the bodies had been removed they would close the area, leaving the builder team to make safe the reaming structure.

Charlie's interest was more the building opposite. He walked the length of the street, although carrying a Dutch Police neck ID pass; he looked at odds with the other young detectives working the scene. He turned at the corner and edged around the rear of the building listed as a safe house for Taqi Al-Wahid. He found the rear of the tall house easily, checked the damaged rear entrance and the building work which had been hastily started after the transit crashed through in the rescue of Yaheem. He edged past the frame work and piles of rubble and new brick pallets. Easing into the house he loosened his revolver catch. He listened but there was no sound. The stillness was eerie. He cleared the empty ground floor and then thought he heard a click from above.

He flattened himself against the wall and stepped sideways. At the splintered door he looked to the stairway, again a click of metallic value. He slipped off his shoes and stepped onto the lower stairs. Listening every three or four seconds he trained his eyes upwards searching for movement.

At the top of the stairs there were 3 doors, the stairway continued upwards. He backed towards the first door, covering the other two and the hallway stairs with his gun. The first room was empty, three single beds and evidence of a hasty departure. The middle room was also empty, much the same condition, the smell was offensive.

There it was again, that odd metallic click. It came from the third room of the three. He was too old for the 'knock and roll in tactic,' gun raised and the villain sitting in the middle of the room, an easy target.

"Come out you bastard, there are 6 of us."

A smothered female voice groaned.

"Oh Shit." He pulled his stomach in and braced himself for a forced entry. He gave the door his full weight and the unbolted door swung open crashing against the wall. Charlie had dived to the floor and checked the room, sweat pouring from his face. It was clear. He stood and then saw the horror of the metallic click. A slim black girl lay naked on the bed, she was manacled to the bed by chains and a small rectangle of skin had been stripped from her, close to her left breast. Her face was bruised and the fear was like nothing he had ever seen before. He removed the tennis ball from her mouth and loosened the chains, her fear had not subsided and she was shaking like a terrified child. He threw a coat around her but she didn't seem to understand him. He dialled Bernart but his battery warning bleeped and 'no service' flashed onto the screen.

He ran to the window, pulling back the sheets covering the glass he opened the window and yelled to the Policemen in the street. "Can you get an Ambulance and Inspector Gris who is in there?" He pointed at the Pink building.

With the girl sedated and on the way to hospital the two Police officers searched the rest of the building, nothing was found although the gruesome basement scene brought condemnation from officers of all ages. The room was set up like an operating theatre, sharp instruments vied for space with ugly metal utensils and blood stains were everywhere. This was not a clinically clean room and once the forensic people had taken it apart, they would need to fumigate the whole house.

Little information was gleaned from the few papers lying around the house, evidence of female abuse was, and in abundance.

A Dutch Policeman walked into the kitchen area. "Inspector Gris?"

"Yes." He turned.

"Insha'Allah just claimed responsibility for the bomb opposite."

Charlie Holmes looked at his French colleague. He shook his head. "No, something is wrong here. This ain't the mad Saudi, way beyond his sophistication level. Bernart, I think I need to get back to London."

"Thanks for your help Charlie, it has been invaluable. Great working with you as usual. Why don't you bring your wife over for a weekend, when you get some leave?"

"In Scotland Yard vernacular, 'leave,' is something you do in a box Bernart!"

Bernart laughed "Tell me Charlie, do they ever call you Sherlock at the Yard?"

"Not to my face laddie!" Bernart looked at his chiselled face, and understood.

Chapter 56

Paris, France.

The Policeman who called at Jacque Martell's large Paris mansion, took Coco into one of the smaller rooms, Ingrid was allowed to accompany her.

The kind faced female, explained Michel's body had been discovered in the ruins of the house in Amsterdam.

The senior officer with her told her of the tape, and the background they had on her partner. Police had evacuated the current owners of the house on Rue Mendel. They were shocked to hear the Police were going to knock through to the cellar, having been told, by the top Paris Lawyer, they purchased the house from, "There was no cellar, and all that was under the house looked to be the well constructed foundations"

A long weekend's work uncovered 11 young female bodies and the small body of Rose Palatt.

Forensic later concluded they had all been skinned.

Her revulsion of the facts did little to alleviate the pain she was suffering and Ingrid gently asked" if they could have a little privacy."

The officers departed, spending a few minutes with Jacque before doing so. A police guard was placed at the end of his private drive, and they had direct access to several numbers.

Jacque had called a Doctor friend to come round and offer Coco some medicine.

Coco cried a lot during the morning and Ingrid was pleased when the doctor finally arrived. He talked with Coco at great length and left her with his card and some medication to help her sleep.

Ingrid walked in the room as he departed with a try of coffee and snacks.

"My god Ingrid, what a mess, what a mess."

Her mobile rang and Ingrid answered for her. "Is she there?"

"It's Bjorn again." He had called several times during the last hours, Ingrid noticing the lift he gave her.

Coco smiled, "Has he changed his name?" She took the phone from a bemused Ingrid.

"Hi Bjorn Again, that's what I need."

"What" he questioned.

"Ha. To be 'born again.' I seem to keep fucking up this time round."

Her voice sparkled for the first time in 48 hours...

Chapter 57

London, England.

Charlie Holmes walked in to his office, the desk was piled high with files and documents and a small group of 'post it' notes, with scrawled messages. He was dishevelled and overtired.

He dialled the Commissioner direct.

"Charlie, Sir. Just back. Need to talk when you are free.

"Come up now Charlie."

Charlie walked the senior man through the last few days. He explained he was concerned the Insha'Allah issue was serious but felt there were other 'forces' at play. It was something he had rattled on about for months, without some credible evidence other than a seasoned coppers nose. In modern Police work, the coppers nose was not in the manual.

"Why would they film it?"

"That is my point Sir, they are not techno people." Charlie loved the word and it usually made older colleagues laugh when he used modern jargon.

The Commissioner laughed, as expected.

"And you are Mr Gates eh?"

"Yes Sir, that's why he's called Bill, he's one of us really." He felt good to relax in such Police Royalty. I could do with a' team' Sir; we need to work cross Europe. I have a bad feeling on this one."

"How many?"

"Five or Six."

"I'll give you three."

"Done." They both new the haggle was Political fodder, to show any post event enquiry, and confirm they reviewed the matter in great detail, and agreed on a select minimum force.

"What a load of bollocks." Charlie said.

"Yes, but there are good bollocks and bad bollocks Charlie, you go and find the bad ones for me. Good luck."

"I would like Ken Robson, Ameer Al Jamal and Carol Murray."

"OK. He buzzed his PA. I will organize that, effective immediately."

"Thanks. Sir. Any more crap from the PM."

"You seriously want to know? The skinning video was on TV all over Europe, the public anger is at an all-time high and Etherington is looking for a scapegoat, we have no idea how the tape was released. The girl was the ATD Aussie lady; did you know? Brave girl."

"No, I didn't." He shook his head; it was a lie. Sixth sense had told him that was the case, but sixth sense was not in the current Police manual either.

"I'll have the 'wooden tops' putting up "SCAPEGOAT WANTED "posters all over the borough Sir. Should do the trick."

The laughing instruction to leave his office, was to the point, and delivered with the full Commissioner volume.

Chapter 58

Paris, France.

Bjorn arrived at Jacques house on time, a rare gesture from the man. Coco ran to greet him and they embraced a firm grip from her as she pushed into his body. They sat together chatting; he constantly reassuring her things would get better.

Ingrid and Jacque joined them.

Bjorn was in a sober mood and Jacques fear of dinner, in his palatial home, with the mad man of Rock, would end with his vintage Rolls Royce flying through the night air, drowning in his Olympic sized pool. His fears quickly subsided as Bjorn chatted about business and life, with equal knowledge. He was surprisingly up to date with the Cognac and Champagne House's latest ventures. Jacque changed his opinion of his guest, exactly as Ingrid had said he would.

The love affair between Ingrid and Jacque had spiralled very quickly and she was trying hard to slow her feelings for the handsome, wealthy tycoon.

He was struggling with the same matrix and even took to a 'consultation,' over an extravagantly expensive lunch with his psychiatric friend; the highest rated in her field in France, Professor Eileen Muroi.

She said, "You don't really need me, just go for it. That'll be $500 please."

Later that night, as his housekeeper served dinner,

he told Ingrid, "The lunch and fee, albeit a joke, topped $1300."

Ingrid seized the opportune moment, when a man is not quite able to make that awkward question, for fear of rejection, and lack of a sensible plan B.

"You mean I get to sleep in Daddy's bed tonight?"

He smiled.

The housekeeper blushed, and hurried from the room.

Chapter 59

London, England.

Charlie Holmes assembled his new group in one of the vacant incident rooms on the second floor at Scotland Yard.

"OK, guys, this is the SP. We have a Middle Eastern fruitcake running around Europe, he is also being credited with various bombings, Australia, second one last week, Kenya and Amsterdam at the weekend, although my gut," he patted his beer belly, "feeling tells me this ain't kosher."

Everyone nodded.

He flipped open a wall chart and grabbed a large marker, writing names and a chart type diagram on the wall. The lines led to France, Holland, Australia and London. He entered dates and other notes, times, bomb size.

They spent the morning challenging the norm, trying to build a segmented case into a whole. It was not positive.

"Guys, I have permission to pass this on to you, strictly confidential of course but you all know me and how I work, any leaks and you will be gone. Period. These recent bombs are not the usual Semtex or fertilizer bombs; this is a new sophistication we have only seen once on mainland Britain, the McBomb at Gatwick, four years ago. The bomb is made of liquid, highly volatile to transport and with the required techno gadgetry needed it costs a bomb as well." The Police humour worked well with the group. "The boffins at Morrison House reckon the McBomb was as small as this." He planted a small phial on the table.

The gasp was unanimous.

"My take on this is someone is setting up Taqi Al-Wahid, why I have no fucking idea and how, I think they are credit calling his name to upset the public. This could be the Israelis of course, not the first time but we have no proof or even a lead. See, I get you all the good jobs."

The group sat together all day and worked on a planned project to try and find clues. The work detail was divided into the 3 Countries mentioned, outside of the UK with Charlie remaining in London as control. He would work from home.

Carol was to take Holland. She was unkindly referred to as 'big boned' within the ranks, a no nonsense detective who had attained the rank of Det.Inspector. Ameer Al Jamal was Iraqi born but moved to the USA aged 3. He joined the New York Police force before moving to England to marry; His language skills were highly sought after in the Met. He would go to France. Ken, or Barbie as he was called in Police circles, would work with the ATD in Australia. Ken's was divorced and his flexibility never an issue, he had the kind of male temperament the Aussies would find agreeable

Charlie gave them all start points, from there you take the decisions, you are your own control tower, so don't screw up.

"We have someone very violent out there, and it may well turn out to be this bloke or blokette, they call the Magician.

The murmur was a nervous one.

Chapter 60

London, England.

Bjorn's entrance through Heathrow was spectacular. Hundreds of ShitBand fans had filled the terminal for hours, singing their songs but the female fans now had a leader, Star Buck. The 'Mercedes 'song' had become a 'chant' for the fans and then the burst into a stomping, synchronized pencil jumping as they revved up the noise, it was all wonderful in Bjorn's eyes.

The Bomy, 'Tomorrow 'fashion label, had rushed out the new jeans, Dina had added her design flair with a star shape cut out at the side of the knee break, they were running flat out trying to produce them in sufficient volumes, the price did not matter, and a black market trade opened instantly.

Dina had warned, "These will be a quick fashion burst and then over." They intended to capitalize on the moment.

The group totalled nearly 60 people and the Press conference was dominated by talk of the Starbucks legal challenge, now in its 11th day. One tabloid in England had run a front page headline "BJORN TOLD TO BUCK OFF." The accompanying picture of Bjorn protecting a semi naked Star, was a mock up, another idea fuelled by the Rocker.

Melanie Preston had not seen the newspaper. Another part of Anita's PA job description.

They arrived to more chaos at the famous Abbey Road Studios, in St John's Wood, a stone's throw from Paul McCartney's London home. Star's pleas to make a 'house call' were rejected by Bjorn.

"I don't think Sir Paul would like 60 guests unannounced or even *announced.*" he joked.

"We got work to do children, the World awaits us."

They poured into the Studio, adding to the atmosphere from outside, already beyond anything the band had created, even in their very early days.

Bjorn smiled to himself, "You can feel the energy here, this is gonna be great!"

The session lasted 8 hours, well into the early hours of the morning, but the results were beyond his expectation. The 4 tracks would be re mixed over the next few days and then the 2 singles released simultaneously, both double sided issues. The new version of 'keys' had been extended to 11 minutes, and had the whole crew and studio session people in raptures.

Melanie had left after the first hour and was at the hotel waiting for Markku to arrive. They had a lot to discuss.

Chapter 61

Paris, France.

Rani was excited to be meeting Coco. He was not so keen on her driving the enormous H1 Hummer into the centre of Paris.

The vehicle, now painted white, carried the same bold chrome signage as the coffee houses, welded on to the exterior. New 26inch chrome wheels had been imported from the USA, adding a rapper's signature to the bling car.

Coco loved it.

The journey talk was about Michel, she was moving forward and Rani was pleased she was not in a down beat mood. Michel Palatt's remains had been returned to Paris and a private funeral had taken place away from the Press storm. Coco had attended, but felt little pain.

The drove to her office, which was buzzing as usual. The walk through the crowded open plan rooms was her first return to work since the news regarding Michel had broken. The staff cheered her and wolf whistled her 'son,' their way of saying we love you Coco. She smiled and returned the feelings.

"You have great staff Coco; they are a credit to you."

"I know; they make the difference."

Delina had her office arranged perfectly and the pile of post was not as big as she had feared it would be. "I gave some to Suresh to deal with and Caroline took care of daily matters if I was unsure."

Coco thanked her and asked for a quick meeting with the usual update crew. The meetings were called VESPA meetings, volumes, expenses, stock, personnel and attitudes. Each manager would give a maximum 3 minutes on his, or her departments key indicators, giving her a quick overview. If there was something she needed to delve into more Coco was able to arrange a one to one with the manager concerned and avoid tying up everyone, which is often the case in so called 'Management Meetings.'

Rani had an hour to chat with Coco about the ELG tests on animals. He had rehearsed the words so many times, hoping to make a little drama as he built towards the most exciting announcement of his life. He crumbled as soon as she questioned his opening words.

"Rani, I can see you are about to explode, get to the point."

He grinned, and burst into passionate eulogy over the remarkable early results. "The 5 dogs we rescued form the local vets, 4 of the 5 are still alive and within 10 days we hope to reunite them with their owners. All 5 dogs had terminal cancer."

He paused as she repeated the word "Terminal?"

He continued, "It is pretty common, especially in older dogs. Fifty percent of dogs over the age of 10 will develop cancer at some point. From malignant lymphoma, which is a tumor of the lymph nodes, mast cell tumors, which is a form of skin cancer. There are mammary gland tumors, or breast cancer, and soft tissue sarcomas. Bone cancer is common in some breeds.

Coco was motionless; he talked with a doctor's confidence for 25 minutes as she absorbed the findings.

"And how difficult has the process been."

"Very, the work with the 5 dog trial occupied 20 people round the clock, they slept on the job. It is still the gathering of the end product once it starts to evaporate, we have 95% loss rate still."

"Can you imagine the impact if this can be harnessed, and repeated with humans?"

He leaned forwards, "Coco we are testing humans, only with those who have literally days left and who are in the worst pain imaginable. We started 2 nights ago, but this is sensitive information in the extreme. It is also illegal."

There was a silence. Her PA buzzed, "The VESPA teams are here."

Coco turned to Rani. "Sit in on this, you may find it interesting. Let's continue our chat over lunch."

"Somewhere very French would be nice." He moved away to take a side seat around her wide desk.

Coco buzzed Delina. "Book a table for 3 at Madam Lille's for 1.30 today. Call Ingrid and tell her to come."

He copied her request, "Madam Lille's? I meant French food."

The Vespa team filed in and introduced to Rani. In their usual street banter, they openly talked about him as if he was n't in the room. Caroline bullying her way to a seat next to him.

Coco laughed to herself at her boldness. "Not your type Caroline."

Chapter 62

Amsterdam, Holland.

DI Murray had been assigned a Dutch liaison officer to work alongside her, Jodie Van Griet, young, inexperienced but street sharp, just the type of young girl Carol liked to date of a weekend.

They visited the condemned Pink building and studied the area behind. It started to rain as they walked round to the building opposite, hoping to get inside. Jodie pulled rank of office on the 2 young rookie officers guarding the front door.

Inside the sordid house had been 'cleaned' by the forensic squad. Odd papers scattered across the floor and few pieces of remaining furniture.

"I would like all these," Carol pointed at the papers, "collected and we can run through them later at my hotel, or your office if you prefer?"

The innocence of youth did not see the potential of their being together in the same bedroom. "Let's use your place; it will be quieter and less distraction."

Jodie made a call and 15 minutes later a van arrived with civilian Police employees to gather all of the written material into boxes and to take to the Hotel Seven One Seven. Jodie acknowledged the up market hotel.

They spent some time in the basement room, hardly talking but sensing the human atrocities, which had befallen so many young girls.

"Are you able to talk to any hookers in confidence, not the programmed shop face ones, those who work freelance, no pimps?"

"Yes I can. Now?"

"Sooner than later."

Jodie drove her VW Passat to a run-down estate, mostly Moroccan immigrants and a few Somali new comers. She walked towards a 10 story graffiti strewn building, clothing hung from the balcony spaces, fighting for space with bicycles, old washing machines and dead plants. Carol looked up towards the top floor. "Looks like Benidorm." She joked.

Jodie had her gun loose by her side; Carol followed the local ritual of safety in bullet numbers.

On the 6th floor they found door numbered 17. Jodie knocked and waited. She knocked again this time adding the name, "Sandy."

"Who is it?" The weak voice seemed to be on the other side of the door, inches from the two Police Officers.

"Jodie, APD."

"Fuck off, I ain't working anymore."

"Just need a chat Jodie, worth a couple of bags."

Carol frowned not quite getting the slang.

The door opened a few inches, who's the gorilla?"

Carols fist hit her just to the right of her left eye, she fell backwards into the flat as Carol barged through the door pinning her to the floor.

"Hi, my names Carol and you pissed me off, so let's stop fucking about and sit down for a quick chat." She did not intend staying too long.

Jodie stood by the door, a shocked look on her face.

Carol turned, "Get in before, someone decides to help this piece of shit."

The door slammed and they walked into her tatty lounge. A black cat with yellow eyes had commandeered the best chair, the room smelt of stale urine and alcohol.

"Now answer this nice young ladies question, and we will be gone." She pointed to Jodie to take over.

10 minutes later they had a name and address of a girl who escaped the Taqi Al-Wahid house. Jodie passed her 2 small bags as they left.

"Was that what I think it was?" Asked the British cop.

"Currency here Carol, money is no good to them anymore."

"Fuck me."

Jodie was walking behind her well-built frame when she made the crude comment. She studied her bottom, enjoying the way it moved when she marched. "Maybe."

They crossed the City centre to a more upmarket area of Amsterdam, large detached houses boasting 4 and 5 cars on the drive, Jodie turned into a long driveway, and pulled up beside a Ferrari.

"Wow, this is a little different to the slum we just visited." Carol checked the car registration and would get Charlie to log it later.

An attractive woman answered the door. "Hello Jodie." The pair shook hands." What can I do for you?"

They sat in her large kitchen, an expansive and stylish designer area with very little evidence of cooking.

Jodie asked her about the Taqi Al-Wahid house.

"Sure we did a few weeks there, bloody odd character the tall bearded one, needed sex almost hourly, my girls were earning fortunes, but then the stories starting feeding back to me and I pulled the contract. I went to see him, he liked to keep me as his special one, like I said, bloody odd, my charms are top notch, but the figure is heading south and he had his pick of 20 beautiful girls to play with. He insisted he wanted to include the French guy in the party but I refused as he was weird, I had crossed his path before. I was n't surprised when I heard that shit on the news. Friggin' weirdo."

"How did they know each other?" Carol speaking for the first time.

"Carol." She offered a hand.

"Hi Carol, English eh? Alana Kosic." They shook hands.

"He knew of the Frenchie from way back. I am not too sure, but maybe 12 or 13 years ago. There was loads of talk around the time about a mad bastard who tried to skin a girl in Paris and loads were going missing. The cops didn't bother much, because they were all mostly illegal imports, and on the game.

I was lucky to get away, a huge slice of luck really." She pulled her top down revealing her breasts," he started here. She pointed to a faded rectangular shape, beside her left breast. "I had surgery but you can still see the outline. Fucking hurt when he did it I can tell you. Managed to hook him in the manbrains with my right leg and he went down like ton of bricks, followed up with a mace shot in the eyes, I can remember his screams, he put a tennis ball in my mouth when he cut me, but I wanted to hear his pain." She pulled her top up covering the light scar.

"Taqi Al-Wahid asked me about the scar one night and I told him the same story, he was fascinated and it became an obsession with him. As soon as he arrived in his flashy Porsche I pulled everyone. One of my girls went freelance as she needed the money, that was her they found skinned in the city."

"Did he ever mention anything about a 'spectacular' to you?"

"Did he Carol? He always talked about blowing up this and blowing up that, we called him Guy Fawkes. He never stopped going on about a spectacular. He could do with a spectacular of his own, small prick syndrome I reckon."

"Have you any idea where they all went?" Carol, hoping for more from the woman.

"No. Just the one thing, he was always asking me if I knew any pilots. I do of course, but I ain't gonna introduce any of my private punters to that fruit cake. I love doing people in uniform." She teased.

The meeting was over and Jodie walked towards the car. As Carol shook hands with Alana she whispered, "I have a really nice young lady free tonight if you are interested."

Carol smiled. "Busy already." Slightly disturbed the woman could tell.

They drove back into the centre and her Hotel. The 5 boxes of papers were sitting in her room when they arrived and they started to collate them into groupings.

There were a number of brochures from Flying Schools dotted around the East Coast of America, Carol segregated them to forward to Charlie. Airline timetables, printed from the internet were the only other items of interest. Huge amounts of take away menus made them both feel hungry.

Carol called Charlie with the day's feedback and added the Ferrari and the information about Michel they had picked up. She also mentioned the Airline timetables and the flying lesson brochures.

They both worried Charlie Holmes.

Chapter 63

Paris, France.

Ingrid was already seated in the wall section at Madame Lille's. Rani sucked air in theatrically as he entered the crowded bustling room.

"Jesus, this is what I call French atmosphere Coco."

Kisses all round from the proud owner, and they pushed their way to the table. The light conversation pleased Ingrid, seeing Coco back on the road to a normal life was a bonus.

"Are you coming to New York at the weekend Rani? She asked.

"New York? No what's happening there?"

"Coco, surely you have invited Rani, especially now he is single."

"In the madness I have forgotten to send any invites."

Ingrid laughed. "I did them for you with Delina, but I didn't know Rani was coming to Paris. Come on Rani, take an extra couple of days out, it would be fun, you need to see the' Top Hat Apartment,' it will blow you away." She giggled. "That's not rude is it?"

The room was heaving and the waiter finally returned with the food, Ingrid had milked the barrels of red wine, but Rani had preference for a bottled beer. The waiter placed the tall thin glass in front of him and leaned over tipping the beer vertically into his glass. The froth exploded into the highball style glass, as the waiter placed the half empty bottle on the table, he lifted Rani's frothing glass and banged it on the table, the froth ran up to the lip of the glass and stopped.

Rani stared at the glass of beer as the froth subsided.

"Did you see that?"

"What?" Coco busy getting updates on the consummated love life of her friend.

"The way he poured the beer, upright, straight in, bang."

"That's the French way Rani, arrogance and flair. None of this painstaking wait whilst they caress the beer into the glass, ends up like a brown glass of coke."

"No, Coco, the problem we have with ELG is the foam or froth, whatever you call it, does not rise quickly enough by volume. Smaller amounts in a narrow combustion tube may help. I have to call Japan." He looked at his watch.

"Call later Rani, this is lunchtime. Chill."

He eased off, but his mind was elsewhere.

Chapter 64

Fontainebleau, France

Doctor Clement greeted another Scotland Yard detective named Ameer Al-Jamal.

"I have bad news for you I am afraid. Mrs Palatt has relapsed into her coma situation and has returned to the wall, I did inform Inspector Gris."

"Yes I know Doctor; I just wanted to see the woman and this place, just to build a bit of background to the tragic case involving her husband."

"Feel free to move around the main areas on your own, if you want to see her room please make sure you have someone with you, regulations I am afraid."

"Thank you." Said Det.Inspector Al Jamal, in fluent French.

Ameer walked through the corridors, passing rooms where patients lay on their beds, some waved to him, others smiled, some shouted abuse but he did not feel threatened. He saw her, standing less than 18 inches from the wall; face alight with facial tones mirroring the words. He watched for 15 minutes as she sung every song with real meaning, her voice was gentle and she mostly recited the ballads. No one seemed to mind the noise as it struggled for air space with the TV, now on full volume high on the wall. A patient dialling with the remote, adding to the dissonance.

A male nurse brought him a coffee and biscuits on a

tray. He was not sure what he could do here, it was just a tick on a long list of boxes.

He asked the nurse if he could see her room and he walked him along the corridor pointing at her tidy bedroom. He looked around without touching any of her personal belongings. He walked around the bed and noticed a calendar on the inside of the open cupboard door at the side of her bed. He looked at the picture, it was of Paris. He then looked at the day boxes; everyone was crossed through, except for a recent 4-day period, which carried no marking. "Odd "He surmised.

'Odd' in his World, is the same as 'interesting', he noted the dates and returned to the front waiting area, saying goodbye to the Doctor. He did not mention the calendar.

He did include the fact in his nightly conversation with Charlie Holmes.

Charlie made a note, adding, "ODD" across the top of the page.

Chapter 65

New York, USA.

The Martell Jet taxied to the Private VIP entrance at JFK in New York. The watery sun greeted the small party as they walked off the aircraft, into the VIP Lounge, a few steps away.

Coco had arranged a stretch Limo and they sped towards the New York skyline. She was fussing over Rani, enjoying the amount of personal time they were able to share.

They checked into the Michelangelo Hotel, all pre booked and exclusive for the Party group. As they entered the foyer Ingrid was name dropping like a schoolgirl, "Behave." Said an embarrassed Coco.

As she reprimanded her Development Director, an American voice behind them said, "Are you Ingrid Boaden?"

They all turned to see a tall man in a Cowboy hat. "Chuck Delante ma'am. From Dallas." It was spoken as a question.

"Mr Delante, how nice to meet you." Ingrid offered a hand. Searching her memory for detail.

"Aw, Chuck's just fine with me girl. Can we get together sometime, before that mad Swede has us all drinking ourselves silly?

"Of course, will you be around later today? 7 in Barrington's Bar."

"You bet. Look forward to it." He tipped his giant hat and walked away slapping backs of people he maybe knew or maybe didn't, it was hard to tell.

"Who the hell is Chuck?" Asked a puzzled Coco.

Rani laughed, "Chuck is the third wealthiest man in the USA. Charles Maxwell Delante, the Third." He waited in the stillness of 3 faces. "Of Delante Oil?"

"Oh hell, I received an email from his PA before we left. He made an enquiry about renting the Top Hat for his daughter's wedding next summer. I sent him a quote; he wants it for 4 weeks in total. The quote was close to a Million dollars, by the time I added in all the extras."

Coco gripped her hand, "see babe we gonna be big in da Hotels man, in it." The girls found their banter side splittingly funny; Rani and Jacque excused themselves to the bar.

"You know Rani, I think those two sniff glue, or something, it's worse than trying to understand the people on MTV."

"I am with you on that Jacque, fancy a brandy?"

The afternoon was like living on a film set, every time they saw someone it felt as if they were old friends, not the Film and TV image, they were in reality, it became second nature to greet famous music, or film stars by their first name.

In Barrington's Bar that evening they met up with Chuck Delante,

"Gimme a contract to sign, and the deal is done for my "Pipkins" wedding next year, it's gonna be the best wedding you have ever seen, I need a few more additions, but we can chew the fat on them, in business hours, for now friends, let's party!" He boomed above the background music.

Ingrid was ecstatic, her first private mail out had produced a sale immediately; Chucks claim 'a few more additions' would add to the income no doubt.

Suddenly the bar erupted, in walked Bjorn Free, shouting to everyone, a crude four letter greetings for the wealthy Oil man, "Hey everyone the Fucking Cowboys are here," he grabbed Chucks 10-gallon hat and plonked it on his own head, everyone roared with laughter.

Chuck looked 10 years older without his huge camouflage.

Bjorn circled the room, working hard to recognise everyone by name; he reached Coco and the group and nudged her along the leather bench seat, planting a kiss as he touched her thigh. She shivered with excitement. Ingrid winked at her.

It was the first time Ingrid or Coco had seen him without a semi naked girl on his arm.

The bar became a party room, as drinks changed every round, soon the atmosphere was beyond electric and new friends were made by the minute.

As the crowds increased Coco was aware of someone standing behind her, she turned and was face to face with Melanie Preston and Star, a man held her arm in a protective manner.

The moment stalled as Coco was caught by surprise and Ingrid watched with concern.

"Melanie, please sit down and join us." Coco threw

open her arms and waited for the hug. Melanie Preston burst into tears and hugged her old friend,

"Can you forgive me; it was so difficult."

"I have already forgiven you she whispered, I have thought about it and thought about it, I discussed it with Ingrid and we want to be friends, it was out of your control. There is no hate in me anymore, it happened a long long time ago."

Ingrid rose and squeezed between them, she hugged Melanie Preston and looked towards her brother, she formally shook hands, introducing herself as if for the first time, aware of his profession and unable to break any confidence. "I never, ever thought this day would come about, Coco is right, we need to repair the past and all move forward."

Melanie opened a bag the he was carrying, "I have saved this for you, hoping one day we would be friends again."

She passed the frame to Coco, it was the poem Simon had written, 'My really place', exquisite calligraphy by Regular Peter, all those years back. It was stained and the frame damaged by time, but it added to the authenticity of the gesture.

The 3 cried together, tears of love for a man they all knew.

The party went on until dawn, until just Bjorn and Coco remained in a corner booth, her framed trophy proudly next to her.

"It feels like we have been here before" he said, slightly slurring his vowels.

"Did you remember what we did last time. "She pouted the last words.

"Sadly not."

"You bastard." She kicked his shin gently.

"Did you then?"

"40 love."

"Want to try again babe?"

"More than anything in the World." She allowed a tear to escape, and touched his hand.

They spent a lazy day as a foursome, Bjorn had left her room just after 9.0am and their night together was still in her mind.

Ingrid looked as happy and the two were like school-girls swapping notes and giggling.

Rani had called Japan with the new idea and was eagerly awaiting a response. For him, New York was an unwelcome distraction; he willed his phone to ring.

Minutes ticked by and the others could see the anxiety. They chastised the hardworking man, joking about heart attacks and his thinning hair. Eventually the call came. He ran to a space as if hoping for a better cell reception.

"It did, oh fantastic, how much, oh my God, we are getting so close. What about the new tests on the, er, newbies?"

He listened for about 10 minutes and wiped tears from his eyes.

"It is a miracle, you are right. I will be back Monday, I can't wait. Has anyone called Mr Toyo? OK I will. Thank you so much."

He dialled Japan and spoke excitedly to his mentor, the conversation was in Japanese and they others could only pick up the excitement in his voice, as good news. He said goodbye to Mr Toyo.

He breathed hard and punched the air. "It works, it works!"

The girls were jumping around him like cheer leaders.

He calmed and explained," Two of the dogs have no sign of skin cancer after less than 12 days' application of ELG, one of the tumours on another dog, has almost reduced to nothing, with no side effects, to date. They lost one of the five, but 60% are almost completely recovered. Recovered, after waiting outside 'deaths door,' at the veterinary surgery.

He grabbed Coco, the tests on humans are even more impressive, and the skin cancer treatment is almost instantaneous, the lungs are reacting quickly and even the brain tumour patients are feeling less pain and one has spoken coherently for the time in 2 months. I can't mention this to the others."

"I understand, has the compression idea worked?"

"It has speeded up the gathering process by 30% but there is still too much loss for volume production."

They rented a helicopter and the pilot managed to negotiate a full circle of the Top Hat Building, they could see the crews inside the two storey pad, busy for the night's party.

"This will be wild! "Coco promised the 3 other passengers.

The wait to get to the Party via the private lifts was long but the atmosphere was charged and people were back slapping talking about 'last night' and their respective hangovers. Coco reached the 59th floor with Tom Cruise, his new babe, Oprah Winfrey, Tom Jones, Barry Gibb and his lovely wife, some baseball star who she didn't know, but he had to bend his head to stay within the lifts height restriction. Someone called 50cent, who claimed to be Star Bucks 'other half,' sending laughter through the 12-person lift. They spilled into the apartment passing Security, and onto the large newly created bar. The lifts kept beaming people into the heaving room.

Excited guests were dancing to the outrageous Crotchless Niggers, a not so innocent looking group of incredibly sexy African girls. Bjorn waved at everything and everyone. He was in his element.

Chuck Delante bowled into the room, clutching a brace of good 'ol Texan gals, he shouted to Ingrid, this is the one getting married, pointing at the top of her head. Ingrid thought she looked about 17, and dressed like a hooker. She returned thumbs up. "Dance with you later Chuck!" She yelled above the drums and guitars.

After a few outrageous live bands Bjorn took the stage and introduced Coco and Ingrid to wolf whistles and some rude suggestive remarks. Coco leaned over to Bjorn and with a smile said, "We maybe should have done this earlier."

"Ha," he cried facing the audience. "The boss thinks you lot are pissed already!"

Coco wanted to hide but the good natured boos kept

coming.

Ingrid was bag of nerves and the raucous celebrities were not going to give her an easy ride. She began her speech and waltz through her pitch with charm and humour, the killer line "This Apartment was fully booked for at least 8 months" drew gasps and applause.

She outlined the plans and the cities and promised to" answer any questions on a one to one basis." The last statement bringing a loud cheer from the single men.

Rani was deep in conversation with Toni Shawe from the USA division and they walked around together and danced together most of the evening.

"Have you walked the walk?" She asked mischievously

"Have I what." he replied.

"The tube, outside."

"Oh crap, no."

"Come on its fun." She tugged at his sleeve.

They joined the line waiting to walk around the outside of the building. Bjorn had organized for coloured smoke to be pumped in to the glass tube, making a fog for people to walk through; he could change the colours every 15 minutes if guests had a particular request.

Toni Shawe stepped onto the glass flooring; she looked down and squealed in fear, just to frighten Rani. He panicked a little making her laugh, she grabbed his arm and yanked him into the tube. His face was screwed; he was deep in thought. They staggered round the tube, Rani gaining confidence with every step until they returned to the exit point.

He stepped onto firm ground with a feeling similar to stepping from an unstable boat ride. He pecked Toni on the forehead; she pulled his neck towards her and forced her mouth against his, her tongue darted into his mouth. He responded to her seduction and moved her close towards his body. He felt an urge that he had never experienced before.

He pushed her away, I must talk to Bjorn, come on help me find him"

They barged through the crowds, hand in hand, passing a surprised looking Coco in the process. She locked eyes with Ingrid and they both mimed an "oohh."

"Bjorn, Bjorn," they both called his name as they approached.

"Hi Rani, she's hot." A touch of introductory class from the master.

"Bjorn, why doesn't the dried ice or smoke rise to the top of the tube outside? It stays flat lined almost."

"Well let me see," He looked upwards as if in deep thought. "I ain't got a fucking clue!" He roared with laughter. "See that fat bloke over there sitting by the control panel."

"Yeah."

"He is called Beans on Toast."

"Ask him, he's my top man."

Rani thought he was being set up for one of Bjorn's practical jokes, but he had to know."

Together with Toni he walked over to 'Beans on Toast.'

"Er, Beans,"

The man swung round to meet him. "Hello, what can I do for you two?"

He asked the same question. Beans sat him down and drew a small diagram on the back of a Party programme. He rambled on in heady technical jargon "but in essence" he told Rani, "The secret is the pressure going in and the size of the container, in this instance the tube. With a tall shape the foam, ice, whatever will rush to the top, quickly making any hope of achieving any density practically impossible? It's an easy calculation, my 9-year-old kid could do it," He boasted.

Rani looked at the man. "Can I get the calculation from you?"

"You in the music business?"

"No it is vital research in Animal health, in Japan."

"You don't say. Here" He handed him a card. "Email me tomorrow and I will send it by return, good luck son."

Toni did not know why but Rani hugged her tightly as soon as they had escaped Beans on Toast. "You don't know how much that means to me!" He was crying.

She kissed him again and whispered, "Shall we go somewhere more private."

The night was nearing an end. Coco had chatted to Melanie Preston, back in her old house, but extremely amiable towards her and Ingrid. Star was due on with the Shit-Band as the finale.

Bjorn stopped the evening, shutting all lighting for a few seconds. As he did so the tube turned Sapo Verde Green, now neon lit rather than the smoke, the guests' alcohol fuelled cheering drowned his introduction of "The

Best Band in the World, The ShitBand, featuring Star Buck!"

The boys raged through 2 numbers and on Spam's chrome drumsticks triple tap they bowed as Star Buck walked on stage, in a tiny red polkadot bikini. She arrogantly grabbed at the stand, unpicking the hand held microphone, her audience, as famous as any seen around the World,

She waited for Spam to catch the mood, turned slightly towards him and winked. The burst of her gravelled vocals had the audience in attention mode. They allowed her the first 2 verses solo, but the repeat had the whole place singing "Oh Lord won't you buy me." It was an electrifying experience as she was joined with full heavy support by her ShitBand colleagues.

Bjorn had seen nothing like it since his heady days touring with a support band to the Beatles, in Scandinavia back in '63.

Star ended her session with the' Keys' song, perfect to conclude a night full of booze, and whatever else was washing around the apartment rooms, and dance floors.

Bjorn took the stage thanking everyone and then added a little spice to the evening. "For all you fuckers I have a special surprise, there is a mate of mine here tonight, who has been through a rough time recently. And, you fuckers all know, mates are more important than anything."

A large box was moving slowly across the floor, Beans on Toast in his element, guiding the box by remote control. Suddenly the lighting in the tube turned to red, white and blue.

"Where is my best mate?" Everyone looked around. A spotlight beamed into the room and danced with faces of expectant people.

It landed on Coco.

The crowd erupted again, chanting her name. A pathway opened towards the huge box and Bjorn invited her to, "walk it Babe."

She reached the box and he swept her in his arms and kissed her.

"Pull that Babe!"

He pointed at a tab on the side of the box. Coco tugged the blue tab and all four sides of the box fell away, revealing a huge, brand new Harley Davidson Motor Cycle in Yellow and Chrome, it was a mirror image of her '68 Harley. Extra spotlights focused on the beautiful machine.

The adrenalin in her body fuelled the emotion and she let the tears flow. She could not speak for several minutes.

Chapter 66

Newcastle, Australia.

Ken Robson looked across the barren patch of land, which once housed Amy's Tavern, the pathetic HQ of the ANP.

The Tavern had gone and along with it a huge expanse of the surrounding derelict land. The early morning sun tried to improve the morbid atmosphere but the level of devastation was like nothing Ken had ever witnessed.

He spoke to the local residents, those who had remained to re build the community. They talked of the night when the bomb exploded, the instantaneous tremors of wind and the rushing air which followed.

Most were still in a state of shock and field hospitals were still operational.

His Police liaison was a young man named Rollo Martin, just 3 years into his Police career.

"Bloody awful site." His young eyes squinting against the flying dust and brick waste.

Ken nodded. His mood was not good, this was not a War you could fight against, and these were inhuman people who hit and run, cowardly souls in his book.

"This goes on for miles Ken," he pointed to a ridge several hundred metres away. "Beyond that line of tall trees there is something you should see. It is eerie."

They jumped in his Ford Galaxy and drove across the flattened fields. At the line of trees, he stopped the car and they both got out. Ken noticed the difference immediately. "This area looks like it has been cleaned?"

"Exactly, but this is how we found it, almost sterile clean, the residents who survived were mostly beyond the line. They talked of the same wind tremors and then the rushing air but then a mist flooded the skies and passed through at super speed, much greater than the first wave from the bomb blast."

"How far did it travel from here?"

Rollo pointed to the row of mobile homes 100 yards away. "The mist reached there before it just evaporated, come take a look around the back of those trailer homes, you will see the front looks like they left the factory yesterday, the rear still retains the accumulation of years of decay, and grime."

Ken walked the short distance with Rollo and checked the mobile homes; he touched the front of the buildings, which were as he had said, spotless. He smelt his fingers but there was nothing to work with, no residue, no stain, and no smell. At the rear he found the 20 plus years of accumulated grime as promised. "That is fucking weird."

Rollo bent to the floor and scooped a small hand of soil, "come back around the front." He repeated the test, gripping soil from the front of the homes. He held them towards Ken. "Just look at the difference Ken."

"Can I bag a couple of samples; I will give them to Morrison House in London and see what they make of it."

He looked around; the demarcation line was almost a straight line.

"Here" he held his arm out straight, "Is cleaned," He moved his arm, "But here, is as it was before." He shook his head. "I ain't seen anything like this in all my days."

Later that day he called Charlie Holmes with his report. Charlie added the third part of the puzzle to his wall chart. None of it made any sense.

Chapter 67

New York, USA.

Coco and Bjorn awoke late in her hotel room. The remnants of their lustful evening evident. Scattered creased bed linen, pillows on the floor, empty Champagne bottles and ash crumpled in a make shift ash tray.

She lay naked on the bed, comfortable with the man who had taken hold of her life, and released it back to her.

She pulled the sheet up to her chin as he walked from the bathroom, a towel fighting his mid drift. "Coco, in your Top Hat Apartments promise me one thing."

"Which is?" She asked.

"You provide towels with more material, and ways of making you feel comfortable, by being able to tie it around your waist properly."

"Wear the robe then?"

"Too old Babe, I still have a barrel chest to show off."

"And something else slightly oversized."

"Slightly? Come here woman."

The playful moment was interrupted by the phone. Bjorn turned back towards the bathroom. "Cold shower!" He yelled.

Coco picked up the phone still laughing. "Hey Coco, it's Rani, can we talk. I need some mature advice."

"You calling me old?"

"No I didn't mean that. It's, well something happened last night and I am a bit confused and you are probably the only person I can ask about it."

She promised to meet him in Barrington's in half an hour.

Bjorn walked back into the bedroom, face and body expectant.

"You've been '86'd." She was already dressing.

"86'd? What's that?"

"Google it lover, google it! See you at the airport tonight if you want to come back on Jacques plane."

"Gotta baby sit the Crotchless Niggers babe?"

"Oh Jesus." She wagged a finger. "Call me then."

"Promise." He kissed her goodbye. "Next week, be good."

She found Rani in the bar, hiding from the party crowd in a booth. "What's up?" She mouthed 'Cappuccino' at the barman.

He stumbled over his words, an uncharacteristic trait. "I got too drunk last night Coco."

"It was a party, that's no disgrace."

"Yeah but I was on a real high after talking with 'Beans on Toast' about the tube."

"Slow down, I am not following this very well."

"There's a chap who Bjorn employs who is called 'Beans on Toast,' He's a technician, does all of his band set ups and the music co-ordination, special effect and the clever stuff."

"OK, why is he called beans on toast?"

"No idea." He stopped talking as the waiter placed her coffee on the booth table. "I was with Toni."

"Yes, I noticed, bright girl, and very attractive. Is that

what this is about?"

"Yup. I spent the night with her."

"And."

"It was amazing, the sex I mean, just amazing."

"So now I guess you are a confused young 'gay' man?"

"Yup." he choked again.

Coco opened her life to him, how she wished she could take control of the family ties, but that was forbidden fruit. She explained her own sexuality, the growing up part, the experiments, the continual questions she often challenges her mind with, her desires of sex with Ingrid, even now.

He looked up, skin colour reviving itself.

"Just go with the flow Rani, you are not unique in that particular field, enjoy this time in your life, it goes far too quickly to hold debates with yourself."

He grinned, a pale attempt at closure. "Hell, I could never discuss this with my Mum. Thanks Coco. You know, I find you very attractive."

"Walk before you run." She kidded his now smiling face. She leaned towards him and tenderly kissed the top of his head.

"Did you see my present from Bjorn?"

"No, we, er left early."

"A huge Harley Davidson in 'my colours,' Yellow and Chrome,' it will be shipped on the plane tonight.

"That's a bit extravagant, you two look good together."

"Just friends." She lied.

Chapter 68

Downing Street, London, England.

William Etherington's weekly meeting with Her Majesty Queen Elizabeth had not gone well.

"Christ almighty Tim, she thinks I am bloody 007 or something, what am I doing about this, what am I doing about that, and what am I doing about Spurs losing their manager..."

"She didn't say that Sir?"

"No, Tim, that's a little joke, but she might as well have."

"Top Cop and Hum-Drum are due in 20 minutes Sir; maybe they will have some positive news?"

"Let's hope so Timothy, let's hope so."

Commissioner Dennis and Chief Superintendent Charlie Holmes arrived on time and they sat opposite the PM and the Home Secretary, Hilary Beasley.

"What's the update gentleman?" The PM still smarting from his dressing down from The Queen.

The Commissioner invited Charlie to reply.

"There are some leads we are working on which are giving us cause for very serious concern. The boys at Cheltenham are picking up a great deal of 'chatter', Taqi Al-Wahid appears to be planning a spectacular, any day now.

We are sure the skin crucifixion chap died in the Amsterdam bomb, as you probably saw on TV, the coincidence of his wife regaining her faculties for just a day or so, gave us a lead, but we were hours behind the bomber.

She then relapsed back to the veggie state, this is work in progress still, and Ameer is still in Paris, chasing leads.

We uncovered material giving us cause to believe he is planning to smash planes into high profile, or marquee venues, somewhere in the World. Indications are that USA is the most likely target. We have informed the Americans but they seem relaxed about the threat.

We would like to move troops into the major airports here Prime Minister, just as a precaution and confidence boost to the public, likewise with Buck House, here and the 'office' over the road."

"That smacks of panic?" The Home Secretary's commanding voice.

"We are almost at panic mode Home Secretary, the bombs in Australia

have caused massive damage, this ELG-9 is more powerful and a greater threat than nuclear. We have to be aware that any of the powerful Countries could be attacked, this of course includes us."

"So why the threat of planes crashing into buildings, or whatever?"

"We think they may use the planes as bomb carriers, fly a small prop plane into the side of The White House, for example, loaded with ELG-9 it blows the whole thing to pieces. The Americans would be distraught. Likewise, here, the same could happen with say, Buck House."

The room paused for a second.

"At this juncture Prime Minister, it would be a sensible precaution for the Queen to leave London for a week or so."

"Oh, Christ, you don't have to tell her that, I bloody do." The PM sank in his chair.

"Any other good news?" Asked the Home Secretary.

Charlie Holmes shook his head.

Chapter 69

New York, USA.

The relationship between Melanie and Markku had been strained since her revelation in London of her role within GM. In effect she was his senior officer although the organization did not run on such formal structures.

'Pride is not a versatile friend' His pride was hurting, his careful lies during their time together at Sapo Verde, the order to terminate her from Aaron Milan, the order would have been given by the Executive, all of the time she was a part of that hierarchy.

She knew the sentence would not be carried out, but how many times had she thanked him? Carrying on the deceit, or was it deceit, he was not sure what was real anymore. Their relationship was burning in the oven.

They were with Star, at yet another Press conference, when Melanie's mobile rang. "Wait, I will go outside, it's too noisy here."

She ran to the door and walked into the street, bathed in bright sunshine. "Yes." She listened to a long, one-way conversation before saying "Immediately, yes."

She ran back to Markku. "We have to get to East 53rd Street. Now."

He looked at her, "What about Star?" He didn't ask why they had to leave so quickly.

"I'll get Anita to look after her, she can go back to the Michelangelo with the crew, and we can meet her there."

They raced outside and hailed a cab." Quick as you can." She waved a $100 bill in the man's face.

10 minutes later they pulled up outside a block of apartments. She threw the high value note at the smiling driver and together they walked into the plush reception. "Mr Mohammed is expecting us", she told the Concierge.

"8th Floor Madam, Apartment 11."

"Is that the Mohammed I think it is?"

"Yes, Taqi Al-Wahid is here, he called Aaron and wants to talk with us?"

"How the fuck did he know we were in New York?"

"Bjorn probably sent him an invite" She joked. They both had guns loosely at their sides.

The 8th Floor was quiet. They moved slowly covering each other until they were outside number 11. Markku knocked and a voice echoed inside the room. The door opened and the elegant figure of Taqi Al-Wahid greeted the pair.

"You can put those away; I am on my own, well apart from my wives."

In the background, they could see three black girls sitting in the main room, it did not take much imagination to guess their profession from the way they were dressed. "OK, ladies, off you go. See you tonight." He handed them a book sized block of £100 bills and told them, "buy yourselves some sexy clothes."

Markku scanned the room for any danger. It appeared clear.

"Trond, we meet again, I assume this is the famous Melanie Preston I have heard so much about?"

The two were outwardly unfazed by the man's knowledge. Inwardly Markku was still worrying about the repeated leaks from within.

"Taqi." He acknowledged the Middle Eastern playboy. "And what do we owe this pleasure."

"Ha, pleasure. I am not sure you Europeans understand the meaning of the word."

Melanie asked him to "Get on with it."

He toyed with her, "Ah, directness, I like that in a woman. I wanted to meet with you before my spectacular shows. Just for old time's sake." He was testing Markku's patience.

"You have a Bank draft for me then I assume."

"For the ELG-9? Ha, no. I found a better way, much cheaper and as effective. When I say 'found' it actually was *you* Mr Trond, who gave me the idea. I doubt you remember."

Trond looked at him, searching his memory. "No."

"It doesn't matter, I wanted you to know it is soon and you will be impressed at the part you played."

"Get to the point or we leave." Melanie thrusting her anger towards the tall man.

"You are free to leave of course; I would never detain a lady if she wishes to leave."

Melanie had a different mental analysis.

"My friends," he continued. "Have you ever wondered why different countries have their own silly obsession with numbers? The Chines love number eight, the devil, whoever he is these days loves sixes, me I adore the four number, all square so to speak?

"And, your point." Melanie demanded,

"No point, just a tease. When my Spectaculars go off I imagine lots of people fumbling for their lucky ritual of numbers"

"We are leaving." Melanie ending the charade. "You need help; you appear to me to be clinically insane."

They left the apartment. "Use the stairs." Markku's precaution from his own life manual.

They walked two blocks before hailing a cab. They said nothing to each other during the taxi ride.

At the Michelangelo they hurried to their room.

He sat on the bed and started to scribble notes and boxes with joining curves and some straight lines. Melanie looked over his shoulder.

He scrawled in a frenzy, "There has to be a clue here, somewhere, why else would he invite us, he is plotting something huge and wants us to feel part of it all for some crazy reason. What is it?"

Melanie asked the reason for numbers, "what was that for?"

They were still searching their minds and the scrawled sheets of writing when there was a gentle knocked on the door.

"It's only me," said a happy looking Star as she walked in. "Guess who I had lunch with?"

Melanie frowned, "Go on then, some super new band or something."

"Please" She said with distasteful tone. "Only Mick Jagger, that's who I run with babes."

The light relief was welcomed by the worried parents.

"Was he nice?" Melanie asked, really meaning "did he try to pick you up."

"Yeah, he has invited over to his house at the Hampton's tonight. Laters."

"Stop!" yelled Melanie.

Star was already laughing, "Only kidding, you should see your faces. He reckons, I will have a Billboard Number One, this time next week."

They checked each other's faces.

"What's all that?" She pointed at their scribble and boxes.

"Just some plans we are working on, nothing really."

"OK. Cool. What time is the flight tonight?"

"10.00pm."

"Hey Mom, I spoke to Millie this morning in Henko."

"Oh good, is she OK?" Melanie keen to stay focused.

"She is sick man, I mean sick."

"With what?"

"Eh, oh no, sick doesn't mean sick. It means, like, you know, sick."

"That's good; I thought I was losing the plot there for a minute."

"She's sick because school starts in Finland tomorrow, it's like so the worst day of the year!"

"I am sure she will miss you darling."

OK. She danced away. *Laters.*" Her new hip jive.

Markku stood away from the bed. "He said spectaculars, more than one, his number is four. For Christ's sake he is planning four bombs!"

"Fuck." Melanie was already dialling.

Chapter 70

Henko, Finland

They walked back into their Henko house just after 11.00am in the morning.

Star had not slept on the flight, spending most of the long boring journey telling people who she was, and posing for photographs with hungry males.

Markku and Melanie had been told to leave the USA as planned, but to await further instructions, if the spectacular did in fact transpire there. Intelligence suggested no threat and added the belief was that the Playboy had run out of money after his Middle Eastern family cut him off in disgrace. His madness now overtaking reality, the negligent summary.

They could n't sleep however, both convinced he would make some kind of statement of intent to the Western World, where they were not sure but America still headed the list.

They had a light lunch and watched Sky News expecting something. There was a flurry of quick changes to the scripts and links as clearly the TV presenters were aware of some sensational news. Then it came.

A stern faced female presenter spoke without the prompter, ad lib she described reports that a suicide bomber had blown himself up at 'The Statue of Liberty.'
"We now take you over to Sara Mecovski from Fox News, our sister company in the US. Hi Sara, what can you tell

us?"

Sara Mecovski was also out of her comfort zone, struggling to ad lib, as the news broke. "Maybe three or four females entered the statue and detonated their bombs."

Melanie and Markku looked at their TV in horror. "Oh, no." She said silently.

The Fox newsgirl was still struggling with the facts and then the bombshell came. "The Lady is down, gone ..."

Markku held his hands against his head. "Oh Jesus, the bastard has bombed the World's most iconic landmark. It's my fault. We talked about suicide bombers." He watched footage as the remaining part of the Statue disintegrated before his eyes

Sara Mecovski was still talking, trying to contain her fear. There was a great deal of background screaming, people started to panic behind the nervous looking girl. The TV coverage changed, picking up threads from France where a team of suicide bombers had repeated the scenario, smashing the famous Paris landmark of 'The Eiffel Tower.'

Melanie was crying, leaning against Markku, who was in shock.

The TV commentary continued, Sara was replaced as she was finding the emotion too much. Seasoned Dan Harner took the anchor role from a position 50 feet from the destroyed façade; the symbol of the land of the free was now a panic zone. It was Twenty first century Armageddon, live on TV. A woman ran past Dan Harner and leaned toward the camera, "Bastards, bastards." She was led away by other grim faced New Yorkers.

The TV clips were repeating archive pictures of both iconic buildings, anxious news crews, racing to the scenes.

Suddenly the Sky studio in London flashed back onto the screens. A grim faced female looked shocked as she read the words in a slow, uncomfortable voice. "We have just received news that a group of at least 6 suicide bombers have gained entry into Buckingham Palace, and have blown the front portion of the building up. They were dressed in Police uniforms."

The World was in shock and the normally astute and confident reporters struggled to comprehend the three disasters.

A couple of hours passed with other events unfolding live, some true, others fantasy rumour, from sick minds. A fourth set of bombers had been shot dead by the Australian Forces as they were picked up as they charged directly toward the Sydney Opera House building. Reports were claiming many civilians were caught in the cross fire as the terrorists were ruthlessly gunned down. The unenviable decision the Australian Prime Minister had been forced to take. Pictures of his TV address to the Australian public showed him in tears. The same pictures were beamed around the World.

As they sat watching, now joined by Star, they listened to the commentary.

Markku commented "There must be hundreds of people and emergency crews in that …"

His voice tailed off as live pictures showed the devastation of the four buildings. one by one. The reporters assuming the bombers had damaged the infrastructure of each.

Melanie wiped a tear from her face,

"Did you see that?" Markku's face locked to the television. "They all collapsed."

"Terrible." Melanie's voice calm.

He shook his head. "That is impossible, the way they came down, that was ELG-9. Nothing else could do that, certainly not a bomb strapped to a body."

The sky TV presenter, held her right ear, screwed her face as she repeated the words from her director. "The Sydney Opera House has just exploded."

He looked at Melanie. She looked away, tears still running down her face as she walked towards the kitchen...

Chapter 71

London. England.

It had been nearly two weeks since the so called 'Icon Bombings.'

The search for missing people carried on and the sites were christened 'Hope Villages,' they had become shrines, and a place for those who had lost loved ones, to meet.

Gadosh Mitsvah Executive had waited for flights to resume, before calling a meeting in London. Those invited, outside of the Executive were Markku Forsström, Coco Cicorre, Pieter Muller and Aaron Milan. The Executive members included Rani Delaware, Seonitno Toyo and Melanie Preston, as well as the Chairman.

The meeting was in the Grosvenor House Hotel on Park Lane. London.

The group waited patiently for their Chairman to arrive and Markku watched the main entrance from their meeting room on the sixth floor. He noticed a Range Rover pull up followed by a Jaguar.

"I think we may have company, that looks like Special Branch to me."

Nobody panicked.

The Range Rover allowed the Jaguar to pull in front and then swerved to the left blocking any vehicle from pulling up close to the Jaguar. Two men stepped from the Range Rover both carrying machine guns.

"Yeah, that's definitely Special Branch," he informed the room.

Still nobody spoke.

Coco looked around for a friendly smile, nerves jangling.

There was a light knock on the door and a man in a grey suit popped his read round the frame. "She's here."

The woman walked into the room. She sat at the head of the large table and immediately began talking to the audience. She had their full attention from her first words.

"Welcome to London.

Many years ago I met a young lady, Miss Gisela Baumann. She turned towards Melanie, you probably know her as Melanie Preston.

Gisela's brother was a founder member of Baader-Meinhof

Baader Meinhof evolved into an intelligent group of activists who saw the negligence of Governments around the Globe. Unfortunately, the World was divided at the time, divided by Politicians, looking after their own pockets and friends, or divided by religious fractions. Baader-Meinhof were on the right track, but misunderstood by most in power, probably deliberately. We kept the promise to those brave souls and as the years went by we found many kindred spirits, who had the same ambition as us. Not terrorists, but often portrayed as such, for the reasons I just outlined. The status quo suits many powerful people.

As you know we have been working with Taqi Al-

Wahid for a number of years, knowing he had a long term plan, to segregate the Islamic and Muslim World from Western civilization.

Working with him was a strategy we agreed, to be aware of what he was about and to try and reverse any threats to the World's population.

During that time, we have lost several dedicated members of our team, we say a prayer for them and their families.

We also say a prayer for those who lost their lives, in the many incidents of which we were compliant, but a vital part of our plan.

These are victims of an unannounced war.

We built a spiteful image around the negative aspects of Islam; those who could be corrupted 5 years ago will now have a more reasoned argument, to refute such advances. The World will distrust people like Taqi Al-Wahid, not just the Western nations.

Many Countries, including the UK, will wage war against him, it is what he wants, to be a martyr is the highroad to legend, and we must not allow this to deflect from our purpose.

We will take care of the madman in time, if the World's elite prove incapable, or unwilling to do so. When I say unwilling, I mean in the name of humanity, not religion.

Phase 2 begins in a few years. We let the currency of time feed the reasonable minds of the young. We then infiltrate those Countries in the Middle East, who force their subjects to live in the squalor of the Middle Ages.

I make no apologies, you have heard all this before.

We will remove Tyrants and Dictators by working within their number, it may take some unpleasant actions, some unsavoury to our minds, but they are essential parts of the whole. Military action with ground forces and heavy bombing raids will not achieve the results the World needs.

The next World War, and the next Hiroshima, would have come from the Middle East. This was General Seonitno Toyo's assessment, many years ago, and it remains the same today.

We will 'convert' these Countries, Iraq, Iran, Libya, Egypt, Syria from being raped by hostile thugs and greedy swine, into Democratic Countries, where everyone can expect health care, everyone can expect to eat, everyone can bring up the children in a safe and honest environment. A life for every citizen.

We aim to achieve this by 2019. We call it *The Arab Spring.*

Learn this phrase.

Before I depart, may I thank you all for your dedication and the huge expense you have incurred in our objectives. As you know we pay nobody in this organization.

I have been talking with Rani, and Seonitno, a great deal over the last few weeks concerning our development of the liquid bomb, a deterrent device, which will now be mothballed for the immediate future.

However, our clever scientists in Japan have been testing the bi product of ELG-9 on animals, latterly on humans also. The results of the tests are conclusive; we have found a cure for 98% of all Cancers. This is not a hopeful statement, we have saved many lives already, in time we can convince the authorities, this will sadly be the usual red tape stumbling block, but we will do it.

The current treatment of cancer is not pleasant, ELG-9 is as easy as swallowing a few pills each day for a few weeks, no other action is required, the expression of the liquid goes straight to the bacteria and cleanses cells affected within days.

Any Pharmaceutical company discovering this cure would make billions upon billions." The woman paused.

"I now come to the reason to invite the slightly bewildered looking Coco Cicorre from the Sapo Verde Company in France. Miss Cicorre we would like this drug to be supplied through the Simon Boaden Foundation on a worldwide basis. I have pledges in excess of £20million to help us achieve this goal. Would this fit with you? The name will of course change from ELG to something more acceptable, and does not link us with the liquid bomb."

Coco nodded. "Absolutely."

"I must now leave for another, slightly less important meeting, but I hate lateness."

Melanie tapped her phone intercom.

"Robert, would you bring her car to the front. Lady Thatcher is leaving now."

Chapter 72

London, England.

Markku and Melanie stopped in the Grosvenor House Hotel Bar after everyone else had left. He ordered 2 glasses of champagne and made uncharacteristic fumbling comments. He was suffering from an acute bout of nerves.

The 'camp' barman carefully placed exquisite champagne flutes in front of them, wiping any residue from the base of the expensive glasses.

Melanie smiled "Have you got anything to cure a tongue tied man?"

"Another couple of those usually helps," he answered, adding an extravagant expression.

"Two more then please." She grinned.

Markku was still silent, rolling a finger around the top of his glass.

"Jesus, what is it." She smiled with her eyes, blinking extended dark lashes, in a demure plea.

He moved slightly on the stool and dropped to the marble floor, bending onto his left knee. Fumbling in his jacket pocket, he produced a small velvet textured box; a strong grip locked her arm as he slipped his hand into hers.

"Melanie, will you marry me?"

The gay barman almost said, "Yes," such was the emotion.

She looked at Markku and jumped from her stool

screaming "yes, yes, yes. I will!"

Others in the bar cheered, applauding the theatre of his proposal. A bottle of champagne arrived, courtesy of one wealthy witness.

An hour later they stumbled through the main hotel entrance and turned toward Marble Arch. They passed 2 car dealerships, premium brands with immaculate cars, neatly arranged under spotlights. As they reached a side road there was a small one car dealership on the corner. The single machine displayed was a meaningful looking sports car.

"Wow. Look at that!" He sounded like an excited schoolboy. He looked to the signage above the tinted glass window. It read Bugatti; he had no knowledge of the marque.

As he stood admiring the car a Ford Mondeo pulled up behind him. In the reflection he watched the man in a pale high street raincoat, step from the car's rear seats. He adjusted his stance allowing him to check further along the road. No back up.

The man in the raincoat stood beside him looking at the desirable vehicle.

"Thinking of treating yourself, Sir?"

"Not sure."

"It apparently does 235 mph. Sir. You would have every traffic cop following you 24/7. Not to harass you, or anything, just to have the chance to take a look at the car, and see what kind of person would buy such a model. But I guess to a man who earns what you do; it's a drop in the Serpentine."

"Me. Earn, I am retired. Do a bit of work for free these days, but out of the system now?"

"No longer a member of the Magic Circle then, eh?"

"Bit of a closed club I hear, Chief Super."

"Indeed, my Guvnor, said to tell you some of your tricks are very impressive, he also insists you perform outside of the UK in future."

"Oh the old illusions, likes those does he?"

"Loves 'em Sir. Loves 'em."

"Then we both understand, would n't you agree Sherlock."

"Glad about that Magician. Good day." He turned, and re-joined the plain clothes Special Branch duo, waiting in the Ford Mondeo.

"What the hell was that about?" Melanie asked

He grabbed her hand and pulled her towards the door.

It was locked, but a button activated from inside, released the lock, with an accompanying buzz.

The neatly dressed saleswoman approached as they entered.

"Hello, I am Janine."

"That is beautiful," he pointed at the stunning car; it was unlike any car he had seen before, "how much is it?"

The elegant girl, twisted a hand across the air in front of her, palms turned towards the ground. "Depending on the spec, plus or minus, a million pounds, Sir."

He was taken aback. "Does that include the wing mirrors?" He was already pushing Melanie towards the door.

He stomped off, marching along the wide pavement

in front of her, she skipped to keep up. He was muttering in a gruff, gravel tone voice.

"A million pounds for *a car*. The World has gone fucking mad..."

Coco's Story

Story continues in book 4

Loser blinks first

TWENTY03
Author: Tomas Berlin
  Contact: tomas.berlin@yahoo.com
  www.tomasberlin.com
  Represented by
  Big Sky Song Limited
  TOM E. MORRISON
  E: tom@bigskysong.com
  Skype: bigskysong

Printed in Great Britain
by Amazon

23405025R00172